INDEBTED TO THE MAFIA KING

THE MAFIA KINGS

BOOK ONE

BELLA MOONDRAGON

For Alyssa. I aspire to be you one day.

CONTENTS

IN A NEW YORK MINUTE

Eleni

"Baba, I have to leave for class in half an hour," I say as I clear paper plates and cups off one of the high-top tables in the back of The Greek Corner. "I need to change."

My dad huffs a sigh and shoves up from his chair behind the counter. "Yes, *chryso mou*, I know. But your mama was supposed to be done taking inventory by now to handle customers. Can't you wait a little?"

I bite back a frown and nod. He's been looking more and more tired since we lost Christos a couple years back. I love the night classes I've been taking at the community college a few blocks over, but I'm not going to force my baba to wait tables just so I'm not late. I dump the trash into the garbage can in the back.

The bell over the door jingles, and I turn with my customer service smile already plastered on, then freeze.

Frank Lombardi, the broad, sneering mobster who's held my family under his thumb since they came to America, saunters in with a few of his guys. My skin goes cold.

"Georgie!" Frank smacks the top of the counter, and I watch my dad bite down a scowl. He's always preferred his given name, Gregorio, but he tolerates customers who call him Greg. Frank has only ever called him Georgie. "Got the place all to yourself tonight?"

"No, I—" Baba stops mid-sentence.

I flinch as I realize his mistake. Like one creature, Frank and his men turn to me.

"Oh, I should've known little Ellie would be here." Frank oozes past the rows of packaged goods to where I stand by the garbage can. "You look good in an apron, baby girl."

I smooth the polyester black half-apron around my waist and smile.

"And even better when you smile," one of his men calls.

"Bet you'd look best of all in nothin' but the apron." The third one smirks.

My face burns, and I start to turn away, but I catch Baba's eye. As always, when Frank comes in, his dark gaze fills with pain. He hates seeing them treat me like this, but he can't stop them. Not without consequences. And as humiliating as it is to be treated like a piece of meat, I'll do anything to keep my family from facing those consequences.

As I turn, one of them smacks my butt. I can't help it. I squeal loudly.

"You got a screamer here, Georgie," Frank calls over his shoulder. "But with her tits pressed up to her chin like that and her ass wagging, I bet you already know that. I bet she's been entertaining the neighborhood for a while now."

Tears prick at my eyes, and I hurry away into the shelves of the bodega half of the store before Baba can see how much Frank's words hurt. I know how people look at me. I got Mama's height, which is to say, none at all, but the body of the women on Baba's side. Even in my high-necked T-shirt, a sports bra, and loose pants, men always comment on my curves. Frank Lombardi and his men are just the only ones who have the lack of respect to try to touch me where my dad can see.

Frank swaggers back over to the counter, places his order, and receives sandwiches for each of his men.

"Great little place you got here, Georgie." He taps on the counter. "Be a shame if something happened to it."

His guys laugh like hyenas as they finally leave. I exhale and step out of the shelves.

"I'm so sorry." Baba stretches his hands across the counter for mine.

I smile and step forward to take them. His right hand is powerful and thickly calloused from years of working all the different kitchen tools needed to produce the authentic gyros that keep The Greek Corner afloat. His left hand.... I swallow. Back when I was in high school, Baba missed a payment. Frank said he would be kind, since it was Baba's first. Instead of taking the restaurant, he'd only take three of Baba's fingers. I grab both his hands and squeeze. The awkward pinch of just his thumb and forefinger feels like home after all these years.

"I know, Baba," I say. "You can't do anything about them."

He glances at the door then leans in. "It's worse than usual, *chryso mou*. He just increased the protection rate, and I don't know if we have it."

I pale and look at the calendar over his shoulder. This Sunday is circled in red. Only five days to make the money, or we find out what happens when Frank Lombardi isn't feeling so nice.

I scurry into the back of the class, thankfully only ten minutes late. Professor Calhoun catches my eye and frowns, but he doesn't point me out to the rest of the class. I know he just wants me to do well. I want to do well. I pull out my laptop and peer at the slideshow on the board. We're still on advanced HTML, which is fantastic, because learning HTML for The Greek Corner's website was what interested me in computer science in the first place. I've barely missed anything.

"Okay, you absolutely can't tell anyone this, but I heard the craziest thing about this club called Piacere out on Staten Island," the brunette in front of me whispers to the redhead next to her.

I frown. I can barely hear Professor Calhoun. Just as I'm about to shush them, the brunette continues, "They're doing a virginity auction. Apparently, some girls get thousands of dollars just to give their virginity away to some sleaze ball willing to pay for it."

The redhead gasps. My heart drops into my toes. A virginity auction. Between how much time I spend helping at The Greek Corner and how much time I spend with Mama and Baba since Christos disappeared two years ago, I haven't dated anyone since middle school, and I'm not a one-night stand type of girl. I would need a real connection to feel safe.

"You're joking, right?" the redhead asked.

The brunette shook her head. "Nope. I met a girl who did it last year. It's like an annual thing, and the next one's on Saturday."

Baba has five days to make the money Frank needs. Saturday is four days away. Three fingers and my older brother is enough to lose. I scribble down every detail the girls whisper to each other and start mentally shuffling through my closet for something that might be appropriate to wear to a virginity auction.

2

TURF WAR

Eleni

I scoot out of the way of Mr. and Mrs. Behrakis as they leave after their usual Wednesday lunch. Both members of the elderly couple smile at me, and I head for their table to pick up their usual generous tip. I haven't told Mama or Baba about the virginity auction. I know they'd stop me, but I want to contribute to this family too.

The bell over the door tinkles, and I turn. My breath catches. The man stepping inside looks like something out of a movie. His warm, tanned skin stretches taut over sharp cheekbones and a square jaw. His black suit is crisp and perfectly tailored over an equally black shirt and tie. The only element of him that doesn't seem like it was mathematically designed for perfection is his curly hair, which tumbles just a little bit into his night-dark eyes. He looks around as if trying to find something, and his gaze lands on me. His smile is soft and a little cocky, exposing perfect white teeth. Without a word, he sits at the counter attached to the front window.

Mama appears out of nowhere and grabs my arm. "I have something I have to show you in the kitchen."

"But we have a custom—" I squeak as Mama drags me away.

As soon as the door swings shut between us and the main restaurant, she releases me. "Do you know who that is?"

I shake my head.

"That's Dante Cattaneo, the boss of the Staten Island Saints." She pushes strands of graying hair out of her eyes and meets my gaze. "And he is not supposed to be here."

"Why not?" I peer through the tiny window in the swing door at the beautiful man, Dante. He's looking around again.

Baba steps away from the grill. "Because the Lombardis and the Staten Island Saints have been at war for years. Both of you, upstairs, now."

Mama takes my hand and starts to lead me away, but I pull out of her grasp. Dante doesn't look anything like Frank and the brutes he brings in. I trust my parents in everything, but I think they might be overreacting.

"Please, *zouzouni*." Mama looks at me with blue eyes so much like my own starting to fill with tears.

"If he's trying to cause trouble, won't it be less trouble if I just serve him?" I ask.

Baba frowns. Mama wrings her hands. Without an answer, I pull my order pad out of the pocket of my apron and march out to meet this Dante.

"Hi and welcome to The Greek Corner," I say. "What can I get for you?"

"I've heard this place is famous for its gyros. Would you recommend them?" He smiles up at me, and my heart skips a beat.

"Um." My face heats. I've never spoken to a man this handsome. "I don't think I'm a fair person to ask."

He twists to look at me. "Why's that?"

Stupid, stupid Eleni. "I'm the owner's daughter. That makes me a little biased."

"Ah." He nods. "See, I think that makes you the perfect person to ask. I'd recommend my nona's lasagna over any other in the world, but that's because it always tastes like Sunday afternoons in her kitchen. She'd be bent over the marinara pot, stirring to the rhythm of the records she brought from the Old Country." He leans against the counter, and I can almost see the scene he's describing in the pitch black of his eyes. "If I asked anyone else, I bet they'll tell me it's a damn good gyro, but what does it taste like to you?"

"Late nights after we close the shop," I say before I can overthink. "But when I was younger, staying up until closing was a special treat. Mama would scrape together enough fixings for everyone to have one last gyro, and Baba would tell the story of how they almost missed their boat to America because Mama insisted on one last gyro, and Christos would bring down this board game he found at a flea market with half the pieces missing and make up new rules every time."

"And what would you do?" Dante's voice is dark and silky like expensive chocolate in commercials.

"I would laugh," I say quietly. There hasn't been much laughter around here since Christos disappeared.

"That settles it." He leans back, shattering the bubble of memory around us. "I'll have a gyro. And a black coffee."

I stumble back a step and write down his order. When I return to the kitchen, Mama and Baba are both standing at the door, clearly listening.

"What?" I say as I walk in.

"Well?" Mama demands. "What did he say? Was he angry?"

"He was..." Nothing like a boss. He's too young, maybe just over thirty, and far too smooth. He can't possibly be in the same line of work as Frank Lombardi. "Nice. And he wants a gyro."

Baba steps over to the grill. "Nice doesn't mean anything, *chryso mou*. I've heard things about Dante."

I lean against the counter behind him. "What kind of things?"

He shakes his head. "I hear them from Lombardi's men, so I don't know if you can trust them."

"Baba," I groan. "You can't announce that you've heard mysterious things and then clam up!"

Mama offers me a small smile. "She's right, Gregorio. You're being a little mean."

"I'm being responsible. Someone in this family has to be." He shakes his head and seasons the lamb sizzling on the grill in front of him. "I've heard there is a turf war brewing between him and Lombardi. I didn't want to say anything because, if it's true, I want both of you to go home to Parikia."

My stomach flips. "Parikia? Back to Greece?"

Mama's smile disappears. "Is it really that serious?"

Baba adds onions and tomatoes to the sizzling meat and stirs. "It might be, Maria. And I'm not willing to take that chance."

His unspoken "again" hangs in the air between us. Two years ago, my older brother Christos disappeared. We haven't heard from him since, and no one has found his body. After six months of waiting, we buried an empty casket. Baba wants to send me to Parikia, a seaside town I know only through stories, because he's afraid the same thing will happen to me.

Mama nods, and I look out the little window at Dante. A man like him wouldn't start a turf war dangerous enough to displace my family and destroy the dreams my parents had when they came to this country. It must be Lombardi's fault. And if it's Lombardi's fault, maybe the money I'll get from the virginity auction will distract him. Mama and Baba may be willing to give up on America for my safety, but I'm not ready to stop fighting yet.

3

NEVER AGAIN

Eleni

I SCUTTLE down the sidewalk after class on Friday night. Professor Whitmore was in rare form, actually seeming to be interested in what people had to say when they raised their hands, but I spent most of the class thinking about my plans for the night. I have to sneak out. I've never snuck out before, but I've seen movies. My bedroom window lets out onto the fire escape, and I'm certain I can get down from there.

I shove my hands in my pockets. The closer I get to the auction, the more ridiculous it seems. Am I really going to sneak out to Staten Island to sell my virginity? Am I really willing to give that to someone who's willing to buy it?

The skin on the back of my neck prickles, and I whip around. A couple makes out on a stoop nearby. An older man with a bottle clasped in a brown paper bag shoos away pigeons collecting in front of him. A few homeless people sleep on benches and blankets. No one seems to be looking at me.

I rub my neck under my loose ponytail of brown curls. Despite that, I can still feel someone watching me. Or, I think I can. But it doesn't feel like the chills I get when Frank and his men watch me in the restaurant. I still have goose bumps, and it's a little unnerving to be watched no matter what, but it's more like…when Mama used to stand in the door until I'd crossed the street for the bus before school. Like someone is watching over me, rather than just watching. A strange warmth takes up residence in my chest, and I hurry the rest of the way home.

When I arrive, the restaurant lights are already off. My stomach flips. Sometimes Mama and Baba close up early when I have class, but almost never on Fridays. There's too much money to be made off drunk people stumbling in, starving and willing to buy anything you so much as mention. I open the door slowly. Nothing seems out of place. The register is closed up properly, and all the cook surfaces are turned off. But something is definitely wrong.

I creep up the stairs to our apartment on the second floor of the building. The door is slightly ajar, and I can hear voices within. My stomach jumps like I missed a step. Someone's in our house! But then, the voices resolve into Mama and Baba.

"You shouldn't have done that, Gregorio," Mama says in a soft voice I know means she's trying to make sure I don't surprise them in the middle of the conversation.

I hesitate in the middle of the steps. Usually, when my parents keep things from me, they have a good reason. But they were wrong about Dante. He was very polite the whole time I served him, tipped well, and hasn't come back since. And sometimes, they still treat me like the youngest daughter, the little treasure they have to protect from the world. If something bad enough to make them close the shop on a Friday night happened, I deserve to know. I sneak up the final few stairs and peer into the crack of the door.

Mama leans over Baba, blocking my view of him. On the counter next to her sits our first aid kit.

"What was I supposed to do, *astéri mou?*" Baba asked. "Let him have what he wants? Is that why we came to America, to sell our daughter?"

I press my hand to my mouth to smother my gasp. Sell me? That has to mean Frank was here, and he wanted something terrible.

"No, of course not. I only mean you shouldn't have aggravated him so." Mama steps aside to grab ice from the freezer, and I see Baba for the first time.

My stomach drops. Bruises litter his olive skin, and a dark line of dried blood seeps from a cut on his cheek. Mama's already cleaned the cut on his forehead and closed it with a few spidering black stitches. He looks like he's been in a fight with a brick wall. Or Frank Lombardi, a man with as much grace and tact as one. A deep, fiery emotion starts to build in my gut, one I'm not very familiar with. As Mama applies ice to a few of Baba's bruises and he winces, the emotion becomes clear.

Anger. I am furious that anyone thought they could touch my family. I clench my jaw and turn to go back down the stairs and pretend like I've just come in now. I need to get to the virginity auction in time to keep this from ever happening again.

"I didn't mean to aggravate him," Baba said. "I thought he was joking, at first. Our Eleni, marry his Luca? I can't imagine it. I can't imagine a man who thinks children are things to be sold off like brood mares." He spits. "There's no choice, Maria. You and Eleni will go to Parikia."

Luca Lombardi, a man only separated from his father by twenty years of pickling in his own noxious evil. He hadn't been in the restaurant in a while, but I didn't remember a time he'd been in and not tried to touch me. My anger burned brighter. Frank should've never put Baba in that position. My dad would do anything to keep harm from coming to me. Now, I had to do the same for him.

"I'm not leaving you alone, Gregorio—"

I tiptoe down a couple stairs, then stomp back up them. "Mama? Baba? Everything okay?"

By the time I swing the door open, the medical supplies have disappeared from the counter, and Baba has disappeared with them. Mama stands alone in the kitchen, drying her hands on a towel I know held ice to Baba's forehead mere seconds ago.

"Ah, zouzouni." She smiles tiredly. "We didn't mean to scare you. We just got tired and decided to close up early tonight. Your baba's already gone to sleep."

I nod and try to smile like I believe her. I've never lied to my mom before. I've never seen her look so tired before, either.

"You should get some sleep too," I say softly as I cross the room to her and hold my hand out for the dish towel. "I'll clean up here."

She kisses my cheek and lets me take the towel. "You are too good to us. Tell me about your class tomorrow, okay?"

"Okay, Mama." I watch her trudge down the short hallway to her bedroom then look down at the dish towel. A little bit of bright red blood stains the blue-and-white checks, and that hot anger kindles in my belly. Never again. I clean up the kitchen, then head for my room. The virginity auction awaits.

4

———————

THE AUCTION

Eleni

I PUSH the hangers holding my every-day clothes to the side and stare at the few special-occasion dresses I've accumulated over the years. I can't wear my prom dress. The long, glittering baby-pink dress with the lacy sleeves seemed perfect when I picked it out, but I'd stick out like a sore thumb on the ferry. I don't really want to wear my birthday dress. It stops at my knees, so I might be able to hide it under a long coat, but I picked out the yellow polka-dotted dress because it looked so cheerful, and I don't want to think of this virginity auction every time we go out to dinner for Mama's, Baba's, or my birthday. That leaves me with my funeral dress. I pull the black sheath from the closet and hold it up to my body. It is sleeveless, with just wide straps holding it up, and the skirt doesn't flare nearly as much as my birthday dress. Every time I wear it to a funeral, I get a little nervous that people might think it's too sexy because of the fitted top.

Perfect.

I slide the dress over my head then prop a little hand mirror up on my desk to do my hair and makeup. I want to seem sexy, but not too

13

sexy, right? Because these men at a virginity auction probably want innocent girls. I swipe on a soft gold eyeshadow over my blue eyes, then apply one of my darker pink lipsticks. Good. The dusty lip really brings out my cupid's bow...I think. I don't tend to wear a lot of makeup. Most of the customers we get in The Greek Corner are locals I've known forever or commuters who wouldn't care if I was wearing a mascot suit. And Frank.

That anger simmers back to life in my belly, and I pull my hair up into a bun quickly. A few curls tumble down to frame my face, and I cross my fingers that it looks charming. I can't sit around here any longer. It's already after midnight, and I can't spend another day watching my parents endure Frank Lombardi torture. I grab the kitten heels I usually pair with this dress, shove my phone and wallet into a small purse, yank on a jacket, and crawl out onto the fire escape. The night air is brisk, but it's not cold enough to touch the fire inside me. I barely need my jacket as I stride down the city streets toward the subway station. All of my worries melt away. Maybe, after we get out from under Frank's thumb, Mama, Baba, and I will all go back to Parikia.

No. We may have buried a coffin for Christos, but I don't really believe he is dead. Not totally. And I wouldn't leave New York City until I know that my brother is gone, not just lost.

The subway and ferry rides pass in a blink. I get a rideshare to the club address I pulled up on my phone before I left, and the sedan drops me off in front of a glittering club with the name Piacere written in twinkling lights on top. There's a line out the door, but almost everyone in the line is a man. At the very front stands a muscular male in a black T-shirt with the word "staff" on the back. I take a deep breath and pray all the movies and TV I watched were right about how this works as I march up to the bouncer.

"Hi." My voice sounds breathless to my own ears. "I'm here for the, um, auction?"

The bouncer looks me up and down. In case it'll sell my story, I open my coat to show the dress underneath.

He snorts. "Yeah, that makes sense. Head inside. Ask for Carla." He unclips a velvet rope over the door and waves me through.

Inside, loud, bass-heavy music thumps through hidden speakers loud enough to shake the floor under my feet. A long, deep red stage runs the middle of the room, studded with golden poles. A few beautiful women in little more than their underwear spin and twist on the poles, to the cheers and dollar bills of the men in the low tables around the stage. To one side, a dark wood bar occupies most of a wall. To the other, I see a packed dance floor and other, higher tables. I blink as my eyes adjust to the darkness then stumble toward the bar.

"I need to see Carla," I say to the first bartender who makes eye contact with me.

He points me through a door, and I pray I don't have to answer any more questions. This is already overwhelming.

Thankfully, the music is quieter in the back room he pointed me to, and Carla is easy to pick out from her crisp suit, clipboard, and the way nearly a dozen other girls around my age and a little younger mill around her. I walk up.

"I'm here for the auction," I say. "My name is El—" I stop. I'm in a sex club. I probably shouldn't use my real name.

Carla looks me up and down like the bouncer did, then presses a finger to her ear. "Last minute entry, looks to be early twenties, great body, no dress sense. Called El."

I blush. "I'm sorry?"

She releases her ear. "Don't worry, it'll be cute. We're starting in a couple minutes. Drop your coat, and I'll send you out with everyone else. You'll be after Marissa. Come back here when you hear that name. Watch until then."

I nod and drape my coat over the arm of a low, leather couch. She ushers most of the girls back out to the front of the house, and I sit at one of the tables as the dancers leave the stage.

Watching the auction is sobering. The first girl, who I think is pretty, goes for a scant two thousand dollars. When the next girl comes out in a sexy dress, the jeers of the men around me grow almost deafening. Several of them chant for her to take it off, while others holler that she couldn't possibly be a virgin, dressed like that. The girl eventually shimmies off the top of her dress to reveal her bra, and still only goes for twenty-five hundred dollars. I chew on my thumbnail. That's not enough for Frank.

The next girl, a pretty blonde in a white dress that highlights her curves just a little, goes for nearly five thousand. Am I worth more than that? I have to be.

Carla grabs my arm. "El? I'm gonna need you to come with me."

"What?" I lurch to my feet. "Am I being kicked out?"

The rest of the girls stare at me. I flush. I don't even know what I did wrong, but I've just lost the last chance to save my family.

Carla drags me back through the door to the back rooms, but she leads me to a different room along the hall. I don't even look where we're going. I just stare at her face, trying to figure out what's going on. She smiles apologetically, nudges me into a room, and closes the door between us. What's happening? I don't seem to be kicked out, but—

A familiar voice behind me says, "What's a girl like you doing in a place like this?"

5

THE MAN BEHIND THE CURTAIN

Eleni

I WHIRL. There, on an even softer looking leather couch, wearing another pitch-black suit, sits Dante. He smiles slightly as he swirls a glass of some dark liquor and looks me up and down.

"Um," I say.

He stands and prowls closer. My heart hammers against my ribcage.

"You shouldn't be here," he murmurs.

"What?" I blink. "I have the same right to be here that all those other girls do."

Dante chuckles, low and teasing. I gulp.

"You actually don't." He circles around behind me. "Piacere is my club, and everyone knows the Calimeris family—including their charming daughter El—belongs to the Lombardis."

The rage that ignited in me when I saw Baba in the kitchen flames back to life. "My family doesn't belong to anyone. And I didn't know this was your club. I don't know anything about you."

He circles back around so I can see him again and opens his arms wide. "I'm an open book. Ask me anything."

I mean to ask him why I'm back here, what he wants from me. But I've never been good at confrontation. "What are you drinking?"

"Scotch. A particularly good one, if I do say so myself." He holds the glass out to me. "Care for a sip?"

I've only ever had a few sips of my parents' wine at dinner, and I can't stand the taste of rotten grapes. But the way Dante looks at me, like he already knows I'll refuse him, frustrates me. I grab the glass from his hand and knock back a sip.

I begin hacking as the liquor sears a path down my throat. I'm on fire. How was he drinking this and having a conversation?

When my coughing finally slows, I realize Dante is rubbing my back in small circles. His hand is warm and calming, but he's a boss. I shove the glass at him and take a step away. "That's the good stuff?"

"I guess it's a little strong for the uninitiated." He takes a sip and savors it. "If you ever get a taste for scotch, come back. I promise you'll enjoy it more."

"Come back?" I stare at him. "You can't kick me out. I need to go back to the auction. I need the money."

He sighs. "I can't send you back. Someone already bought a night with you."

Relief washes over me in cool waves. I don't know why I didn't have to get up on the stage like the other girls, but I've done it. I've done everything I can to save my family.

"For how much?" I ask.

He smiles. "How much do you think?"

That teasing smile again. I cross my arms. "More than five thousand."

"You're right about that." Dante chuckles as he walks back to the couch and picks up an envelope lying on the arm. "Fifty grand for you to go home and spend the night with your family."

My knees go weak, and I sink onto the couch. Fifty grand. That has to be enough to cover Frank, maybe even enough to get us ahead for next month. But...why would someone want me to just go home?

"You paid for me?" I say slowly.

He nods. His dark eyes burn into mine like he's trying to communicate something.

Dante is a boss. No matter how smooth or handsome or young, he's the same type of person as Frank Lombardi. If I take this money and leave, I'll only be moving who owns my family.

"No," I say. "I'll owe you if I take that."

He sips his scotch and sits on the other side of the couch. "Why?"

"I know better than to accept money from people like you." I climb unsteadily to my feet. "There are always strings attached."

"You're a smart girl, but naïve." He smiles at me. "If I wanted you to owe me, I'd say that. Consider this…a get-out-of-jail-free card. Take the money and go."

His smile, his plush lips parting over his perfect teeth, starts to cloud my mind. But I can't lose focus. Mama and Baba need me.

"I came here to auction off my virginity." I smooth my hands down my dress. "I've made my peace with that. I won't fall into a mafia boss' debt instead."

His dark eyes go somehow darker, liquid. "Then spend the night with me, if it'll clear your conscience."

The fiery anger I've been feeling all night drops lower, between my legs. I didn't know what sort of man would buy me, but Dante is hardly the worst I imagined. This close, I can see the very beginnings of fine lines around his eyes and mouth. Smile lines. Baba said he was Frank Lombardi's rival. That feels fitting, to get my family out from under Frank's tyranny. We need this money.

I take the envelope from Dante. It's heavy in my hands, all cash, certainly more money than I've ever held before. Maybe enough to get Frank to go away forever. I tuck it into my purse and turn back to Dante.

"Will you tell me what the money's for?" He sets his glass on a side table.

"No." I grab the zipper at the back of my dress and pull it down. My good funeral clothes puddle on the floor around my feet.

Dante stares at me with those burning eyes, and I fight not to blush. I knew what I was getting into. A man was always going to see me in my underwear, matching but plain gray because I didn't have anything sexier. But somehow, with his gaze on me, it feels different. He stares like he's looking through me, seeing underneath my skin. Before I can lose my nerve, I climb into his lap and press my mouth to his.

His lips mold to mine, soft and warm and tasting like the shred of flavor I actually got off the scotch. In his mouth, I don't mind it nearly as much. He rolls his hips up into me, and I grab his shoulders for balance. His suit feels like the nice sweaters I can never buy in department stores. He grabs my hips, his hands hot but somehow gentle.

A noise I've never heard myself make before pours from my lips, something low and needy. I start to blush, but Dante pushes his tongue into my mouth. I always thought French kissing sounded awful, but he moves in a way that chases all those assumptions from my mind. He pulls another moan out of me and tangles his tongue with mine.

Distantly, I hear tinny music. He releases one of my hips and pulls away from the kiss to answer his phone.

"Cattaneo," he says.

He listens for a long moment, then nods. "I'll be there shortly."

I stare at him. What?

"I'm sorry." He pecks me on the cheek. "Business calls. Take the money, please." He rolls his hips again, and I feel something hard between us. "Maybe I'll just call in a favor someday."

Gently, he dumps me off his lap and leaves the small room. I stare at the door for what feels like an hour, then finally pull my dress and coat on with shaking hands and leave. I got all the money I could've hoped for, and I didn't even have to lose my virginity.

So why do I feel so disappointed?

6

WALK OF SHAME

Eleni

I SLIP out of the front door of Piacere without looking at the stage, where the auction is still going on, or the line of people outside. People—men—from both groups jeer at me, but I ignore them. The envelope of money weighs down the inside pocket of my jacket. Fifty thousand dollars. I hurry through the streets. I have to get home before Baba and Mama wake. The last thing I want is to worry them.

Only when I'm already on the ferry back to the city proper do I think about Dante. My face heats. I threw myself at him, and he basically refused. I bite my lower lip, still tingling from the heat and pressure of his kiss. I really thought he wanted me. Stupid. Men like him only ever want me for my body, but I could tell he wanted someone with more to them than that. He just didn't see more in me.

Tears bead in my eyes, and I shake my head. Sure, I sold more to Dante than I ever wanted to, but I have the money. Mama can stop cleaning up Baba's blood, at least.

When I arrive home, I lock the door behind me, slide the security chain into place, strip out of my funeral dress, and collapse into bed.

Sleep evades me for a while. I just keep picturing the look in Dante's dark eyes when I climbed onto his lap. In that moment, I felt like a completely new person, sexy and powerful. And he rejected me.

I take a deep breath and try to put the whole night behind me. Dante, his dangerous eyes, auctioning my virginity, they all stay on Staten Island. Everything but the fifty thousand dollars in the top drawer of my little desk.

***

I startle out of my sleep to a metallic sound I can't place. Maybe Baba woke up early and is banging around in the kitchen downstairs.

Something shatters. I sit up. That sounded like glass. And I don't hear any of Baba's furious Greek cursing.

Everything goes quiet for a moment. I slide out of bed and pull a sweatshirt over my nightgown. Then, my heart pounding in my ears, I pull the envelope of money out of my desk drawer and slide it into the front pocket of the sweatshirt. My door swings open quietly, and I grab the nearest thing I think counts as a weapon—one of my computer science textbooks.

Baba stands in the door, clutching a baseball bat. "Go to Mama in our room, *chryso mou.*"

I grab the envelope and start to shake my head. "No, I—"

"It's my job to protect this family." His face turns deadly serious.

I've never seen Baba look like that, not even when he said Mama and I should move back to Greece. Not even last night, when he was getting patched up in our kitchen. Something terrible is happening. The money won't fix this.

I nod.

He steps out of the doorway to let me pass as the security chain rattles. He goes pale, then turns and marches toward the door. Sometimes, when Christos and I were young and couldn't fall asleep, he would tell us stories of his baba, my pappous, and his time in the war. Christos preferred them, especially the ones where Pappous escaped some terrible fate by sheer ingenuity, but we shared a room, so I heard them all the same. When Baba marches to the front door, he looks exactly like he described Pappous, straight-backed and determined to face whatever comes. My stomach sinks to my toes.

I scramble down the hall to Mama as, with a splintering of wood, the door bursts inward. Baba looses a war cry. I open the door to their bedroom, duck in, and shut it behind me. Mama perches on the edge of the bed, deathly pale in the early morning light. I sit next to her, and she takes my hand with a crushing grip.

Someone grunts in pain. I can't tell who. Something smashes. Baba curses at the same moment something splatters, and Mama winces.

"Run, my—" Baba's words cut off on a gurgle.

I shoot to my feet. I said never again. I snuck out in the middle of the night to sell my body so I could protect everyone. What am I doing, sitting here and waiting for whatever will come? Mama stares up at me blankly.

"It's over," she whispers. "Frank wanted you, and that's the one thing we would never give him."

"It's not over until I say so." I yank open dresser drawers until I find a pair of pants Mama can pull on under her nightgown and throw them at her. I'll have to make do. "Put those on, then go out the window. I have to do something."

Baba screams, a pained, animalistic sound, and my skin turns to ice. Mama doesn't move.

I grab her by the shoulders. "I can't lose you both."

My voice cracks, and though she never looks away from the door, she starts to move. That has to be enough. I sprint into the hall. Whatever monsters Baba is facing in the living room will pursue Mama and I. That fact crawls into my bones. They—

No point in saying they. Frank Lombardi will never give up. A hot, tight feeling takes hold of my ribs. Baba screams again, and a smell creeps down the hall. Something overwhelming and metallic.

Blood. My stomach twists.

I race for the tiny bathroom Baba always wanted to redo. He hated the old-fashioned drop ceilings, those little square tiles that gave the super such easy access to our pipes. One time, I was the only one home when the super was fixing the shower. He let me watch him work and showed me a secret. A secret I need now.

Footsteps down the hall. I pray Mama listened, that she left.

I fling open the door to the bathroom and clamber onto the toilet. My feet slide, covered in panicked sweat, but I punch up the ceiling tile I need. Third from the wall, two up. This building changed supers a lot for a while, even got a reputation for it. So the supers installed a box in the ceiling, to leave notes for the next one of the building's weird quirk. I slide open the little wooden box, fold the envelope of money, and stuff it behind sheets of yellowing paper.

The door crashes open. I slide the ceiling tile back into place, leap off the toilet, and misjudge my landing. My heels slide, and I collide with the tile floor, hard.

A massive man I don't recognize looms through the doorway. "You."

I spit at him.

He hauls me off the floor by my hair in a bright burst of pain and stuffs a bag over my head. I scream, claw at his arm, anything I can think of, but he's inexorable. He tightens the bag until it almost chokes me and throws me over his shoulder.

"I'll get you back for this," I yell. "I don't know who you are, but I'll find you, and you'll regret the day you ever heard the name Calimeris!"

"All right, cutie." He smacks my butt a few times, condescendingly. "This'll go a lot easier if you quiet down."

"Fuck you!" My first ever curse word slips from my lips, just another thing ruined on this awful day, and I try to remember everything I've ever learned about self-defense: Go for the groin—not useful in the air; don't get grabbed—too late for that; the eyes are always weak–that might work.

I snarl and claw for where I hope his face might be. My fingers, newly manicured by Mama a couple days ago, catch skin and tear. I hold on and sink my nails in. He howls and dumps me on the nice, tan carpet. Mama was so pleased when we installed it in the living room.

It squelches underneath me. I draw back my hand and find it sticky. The metallic reek overwhelms me, and I just know.

Baba is dead, and I'm sitting by his remains.

"You bitch." The massive man cracks something hard and metal against my cheek.

Pain explodes through my world, and I topple to the side. Another squelch. More Baba. This man, this monster, slams the metal thing into my face again. A second time. A third.

"Regret the name," I mumble woozily.

On the fourth hit, I slip into unconsciousness.

7

WALK IT OFF

Dante

I DROP into my leather desk chair and cradle the hot mug of coffee I picked up in the kitchen to my chest. The virginity auction at the club is usually a great way to make some money and pull new eyes. I show up every year, but I've never bid before. I'm no saint, but women who've never had any kind of sex before tend not to be as…flexible in bed as I prefer.

But goddamn Eleni Calimeris. El, as she called herself, one of the worst fake names I've ever heard. I can't get her out of my head. When I went to The Greek Corner the other day, I was just hoping to rile Frank Lombardi. The dickhead gets reckless when he's mad, so pissing him off is almost always good business. I didn't expect Eleni.

I take a sip of the coffee and allow myself a minute to think about her before I have to do some work. The bun she'd worn to the auction last night made it impossible to think about anything but tasting the skin of her neck. When I asked her what the gyro tasted like to her, her soft blue eyes took on a faraway look that I wanted to dive into, like a pool on a hot summer day. And when she climbed onto my lap last night—

I groan.

Someone raps on the door to my office. Three short knocks, one long. That means Tony Bellini, my caporegime.

"Come in." I straighten the handful of papers on my mahogany desk and open my laptop like I've been working.

He steps in and shuts the door behind him. Even this early in the morning, he looks polished. Crisp navy suit, hair gelled back, a sharp look in his icy blue eyes. I've spent half my life hearing from different women how they want to melt the ice in those eyes.

"You look like you took a swim in the Narrows," he says by way of greeting.

"Fuck you too," I reply.

He laughs. "Seriously, Dante, what the hell happened to you? Carla said you disappeared halfway through the auction last night."

I look at my best friend, my right hand. I love him like a brother, but if I tell him about Eleni, not only will he make fun of me forever, he'll tell me she's not worth the turf war. Maybe he's right. But I don't want to hear that right now, when I can still picture her slinking toward me in that church dress.

"I was with that rat Eddie last night." Not a lie, technically. "Left him in the hands of a couple bruisers when the auction started, but I only ordered one drink before I got the call he'd finally cracked. The auction's good business, but Carla runs it with an iron fist. She didn't need me."

Tony nods slowly. "Anything good shake loose from Eddie?"

I sip my coffee. The dark brew burns down through my body. "He's a rat, but he's a shitty rat. He gave old drop details to a few runners for Lombardi at the docks. Nothing to worry about."

He drops into the armchair across the desk from me. "Funny you mention Lombardi. He's actually why I'm here."

"What, it's not just for my beautiful smile?" I grin at him.

He rolls his eyes. "I'll show up for your beautiful smile when you get one of those. No, Lombardi's making moves. He had a couple of his heavies take out a restaurant owner under his own goddamn protection."

"Idiot." I shake my head. The occasional internal hit inspires respect, but Frank's a loose fucking cannon. Everyone under him is going to assume this is the beginning of a cull, and his protection racket is going to dry right up. He actually has to supply something if he wants people to demand it. "What restaurant?"

"That little Greek place." Tony snaps out a knife and begins cleaning his fingernails.

My heart skips a beat. "The Greek Corner?"

"Yeah, I think that's the one," he replies.

My pulse thrums. Almost every real answer I've gotten out of Eleni was about her parents, her family. She clearly loves them. Hell, I wouldn't be surprised if Frank Lombardi and this hit has something to do with her showing up at the auction in the first place. But I gave her the money. Why didn't she use it?

In my mind's eye, I picture her beautiful eyes filling up with tears, her small, strong hands stained with blood.

I shoot to my feet. "Round up the boys."

"What?" Tony snaps his knife shut again. "Five minutes ago, you were roadkill."

"Call me a fucking zombie if it makes you happy. We're going into the city." I stride around my desk to the massive, unlit hearth against one wall. I pull on the left cast-iron sconce, and the false back wall of the fireplace slides away to reveal the rack of guns within. "I've got business."

"Fuck, okay." Tony stands. "We'll be ready in fifteen."

He leaves the room. I pull my favorite pistol from the rack, close the fireplace, and return to my desk to place a call.

"Who is this?" the voice on the other end asks suspiciously. "You're not already a contact, and nobody's supposed to know this number."

"You're Louie, right?" I smile. "This is Dante. Put me on with Thano."

The young man on the other side of the phone—on the other side of state lines, with the rest of the Coppola syndicate in Jersey—splutters for a moment. Then, he seems to place my name.

"Mr. Cattaneo!" he says. "Mr. Coppola is in a meeting right now, but—"

"Thano owes me." I infuse my voice with a note of steel. "Take the phone in. Put it against his ear, if he won't grab it himself. I'm calling in my chip."

"Yes, Mr. Cattaneo." Eli rustles like he's standing up, and I just barely hear a few knocks.

Muffled conversation. I can't make out anything solid, but there are at least three voices.

"Dante," Thano says finally. "You've got shit timing."

"Who doesn't in this life?" I lean back in my chair and run a cleaning cloth over the pistol on my desk. "I don't intend to take much of your time."

"Not yet, you don't," Thano mutters. "What?"

"Where can I find Frank Lombardi?"

8

PAYMENT

Eleni

I BLINK awake and discover someone removed the bag from my head. I lie on a scratchy couch in what looks like someone's wood-paneled basement, still wearing my sweatshirt and nightgown. A single lightbulb battles against the dark, but it barely reaches the walls. I suck in a breath, and the musty scent of underground combines with just a hint of the metallic stench I remember from the apartment.

The apartment. Where I left Baba dead. Mama isn't here, so at least they haven't caught her yet. Or they killed her too. Tears fill my eyes, and I lift a hand to swipe them away.

Both of my hands move, accompanied by the sharp bite of plastic. I look down. Someone zip-tied my wrists together. And my ankles.

I shriek. Maybe someone will hear me.

A door opens, and several people pound down the stairs. The first, the same massive man from the apartment, backhands me, stuffs a rag into my mouth, and slaps a wide piece of duct tape over the rag so I can't get it out.

"Shut up, bitch," he spits.

The rag tastes sharp and acidic, like I imagine gasoline would. Pain cascades through my head. My tears overflow and run freely down my cheeks. The men who came down with the murderer laugh.

"She is a pretty thing," one of them says. "With the gag, I can already picture her lips around my cock."

The massive man stands. "I've got dibs, shithead. And I'm not gonna waste those on her fucking mouth."

"What the fuck are you gonna do, then, Leo?" the first man asks.

"With a sweet little treat like this?" He grins in a way that makes my skin crawl. "I think I'd fuck her tits until I got good and close, then bust inside her. Always gotta be thinking about your legacy, boys."

The cluster of monsters laugh. I can't do anything but lie there and cry. If I thought the comments in the shop were bad, I had no idea.

The door at the top of the stairs opens again, and everyone falls silent. Slowly, Frank Lombardi makes his way into the basement and to the front of the pack. He puts out his hand, and one of them produces a folding chair from the dark edges of the room for him. Frank sets the chair down and sits. Then, he grabs the zip ties around my wrists and pulls me until I'm sitting up too.

"Don't be afraid," he says. "I'm not gonna kill you."

That only makes me cry harder. I'd rather be dead. I'd rather see Baba and Christos again than undergo whatever torture Frank Lombardi has designed for me.

"That's not gonna work, baby girl." He wipes my tears away. "I've got a hard old heart, and you're not someone who gets prettier when you cry. And anyway, there's no reason to cry. I can be kind when I want to be, right, boys?"

The monsters behind him nod.

"You're here, Ellie, because I've decided to take matters into my own hands." He pats my cheek too hard, more like a slap. "I'm giving you the life you deserve. My Luca's on the hunt for a bride, and I think you'd be perfect."

Nausea churns my stomach. Luca Lombardi again. Baba always thought Luca was the one who killed Christos. With Baba's blood still sticky on my hands, I do too. The monster in my apartment shows that Frank Lombardi doesn't do any of his own work, and Luca's enough of a brute that he might've just snapped on Christos one day.

I cannot marry him.

"It's a good match." Frank leans back. "I'd be honored, if I were you. Luca's set to take this whole operation over when somebody finally puts me in the ground. You'd be a multimillionaire, living in the lap of luxury. And Luca will take good care of you. He likes pretty things."

A couple of the men snicker. Frank whips around to glare at them then turns back to me with a small smile.

"Ignore them. They're apes. Luca may have displayed some…less than ideal tastes in the past, but with a wife like you…." Frank runs a finger along my cheek. "Well, I'm sure you'll keep him in line. Won't you, baby girl?"

I just stare at Frank. The gag bulges out my cheeks. I couldn't say anything even if I wanted to.

"Fine." He sighs. "Someone take the gag out. But just know screaming won't help you."

The massive man, Leo, rips the tape off and pulls the rag out. My cheeks sting. I draw in a deep breath as they all look at me.

"I'd rather die than marry Luca." I spit on Frank Lombardi.

Frank is on his feet faster than I can follow, and his hand cracks into my cheek, knocking me back onto my side. I scream in pain as he hits what must be a bruise left over from whatever they did to knock me unconscious. But Frank drags me up to sit again and pulls my knees apart.

"You're too cute to waste on death just yet," he hisses. "If you won't have my son, fine. You can open your pretty little legs for my men instead." He grabs a handful of my nightgown and starts dragging it up my thighs.

Something sparks in my chest. Maybe, if I can make him angry enough, he'll just kill me. I twist and writhe in his grip, fighting for any kind of distance. He just laughs and holds on. But I don't need distance. Both of my legs are tied together, making a perfect battering ram.

I throw myself back against the couch and bring my legs up to crush his genitals. Frank makes a low, pained sound and grabs me by the throat.

"You little bitch." He looks furious, angrier than I've ever seen anyone.

His grip on my throat tightens, and I barely suck a breath into my lungs. I can feel the bruises forming under his fingers. For a moment, I think the light is going out, but then I realize my vision is just dimming. The monsters around Frank laugh as unconsciousness reaches for me again.

I'm coming, Baba, I think. I'm coming, Christos.

WHEN I OPEN my eyes again, everything is dark. I can still feel the scratchy couch underneath me, as well as the zip ties around my wrists and ankles. My nightgown is around my waist, but my panties are still on, like they only wanted to look. And they've put the bag over my head again, pressing into the ache where Frank Lombardi grabbed me.

I begin crying. This is my life now. I am going to live and die in a basement where awful men use me.

Something smashes upstairs. There are yells and the sharp takka-takka of gunfire. My heart races. Is someone killing Frank? Will they think to look down here?

If they find me, will they save me or take me for their own use?

After long moments of fighting, the basement door creaks open. My heart pounds in my throat. Someone walks down the stairs. I hear a sharp intake of breath.

They rip the bag off my head.

9

END OF THE LINE

Dante

I stare down at Eleni, bloody, bruised, and half-covered. Rage lights in my veins, something deeper and truer than I've felt before. I knew Frank Lombardi was scum. I've touched enough blood that he spilled to never question that. But violating Eleni like this is something new. It's the end of the goddamn line for him.

She stares up at me, and the confusion in her wide, blue eyes morphs slowly into fear. "Dante? Wh-why are you here?"

Fuck. I never want to scare her. I kneel and snap out my switchblade. She flinches, but I can't do anything about that. I slit the zip ties around her ankles, fix her skirt, then hold out my hands for her wrists, struggling to keep my movements slow and calming.

Her lower lip trembles. Her gaze darts across my face like she's trying to guess what I'm thinking. I hope she doesn't. Blood-bright pictures spatter the inside of my skull, all featuring Frank Lombardi. I'll string him up by his guts. I'll make him eat his own cock. Anything that'll show him exactly how badly he's fucked up.

After a long moment, Eleni puts her wrists in my hand. I cut the zip ties and help her to her feet. I just need to get her out and—

Out. Fuck. At the top of the stairs and beyond lie the pile of bodies I left in my wake getting to her. She doesn't need to see that.

"Close your eyes," I murmur, trying to keep the fury out of my voice. "And be quiet."

This time, she obeys without hesitation. I thank my lucky stars and take her hand. She's got delicate fingers, but her palms are calloused. Probably from shifts at the family restaurant, carrying burning trays back and forth. I've never met a waitress without calluses like this. Somehow, that makes her abruptly more real. She's not just the beautiful woman in the restaurant or the back of my club. She's Eleni, a woman who lost her father last night.

Frank Lombardi is going to die for this.

I lead her up the stairs and into the back hallway of the auto shop Lombardi uses as his main headquarters. Tacky, I've always said. But his black-and-white checkered color scheme isn't really benefiting from the blood splattered across it. I try to lead her around the bodies, but her bare feet slide in the puddles of blood, and I have to catch her more than once.

I round a corner, intending to take her outside, and come face-to-face with Frank Lombardi, clearly just arriving because one of his men called him before they died.

"What the—" He grabs for his gun.

Eleni tenses. She knows his voice. But she keeps her eyes closed like I demanded. Liquid rage pours through my veins, but I put a hand up very casually.

"I wouldn't, if I were you."

Frank blinks stupidly. Moron.

"I bought this young woman at an auction recently," I say. "And I don't take kindly to others touching my things."

Eleni sucks in a breath. I force my thoughts away from her. Frank has his gun out, and I have someone I'm willing to get seriously injured to protect. I need to turn this stack of disadvantages into crushing Frank's skull underfoot.

"It's finders-fucking-keepers in this city, you little shit." Frank levels his gun at Eleni. "But if I can't have her...."

A door behind him bangs open, and Tony and his younger brother Sebastian exit, blocking Frank's escape. I left them behind to clean up the small battalion of capos and soldiers in the auto shop itself. Now, I look like a fucking genius.

Frank glances behind him, then back at me. "Maybe you are smarter than your old man after all."

"Keep all references to him out of your fucking mouth." I snarl and knock the gun out of his grasp, then release Eleni's hand to draw my own.

Frank chuckles, and I see red. But Eleni makes a small, worried noise, like she's lost without my touch.

"Open your eyes, El," I say quietly.

She gasps as she does. I can feel Tony and Sebastian wondering who this girl is, why I know her, but I ignore them.

"It's your call," I say. "Do you want him dead for what he did to your father, or do you want to end this and spare him?"

She looks at Frank, who grins like he's already confident she's going to let him live. Then, she looks at me, and I see something new in those blue eyes of hers. A fury as deep as my own.

"Kill him," she says.

I pull the trigger before Frank can reply. He collapses onto a pile of his men, his forehead spouting blood. Eleni doesn't even flinch when the gun goes off. But when Frank finally goes still, she takes my hand again.

"I have to get her out," I say to Tony and Sebastian.

"You sure?" Tony asks. "Seems like she's got the balls to take a few of Frank's fucks out herself."

He meets my gaze, and under his sarcasm, I see real confusion, almost concern. I haven't done anything he couldn't predict in a long time.

I shake my head. I'll explain later. He sighs.

"Loot the place," I call over my shoulder as I walk toward the double doors. "Burn it, do whatever you think will send the right message to the remains of the syndicate. I want Luca scared."

Eleni squeezes my hand when I say that, a mute agreement, but she doesn't look at me. I lead her through the shop itself, littered with more bodies and my men already rifling the place, then out into the Harlem night. She shivers at the drop in temperature, so I bring her quickly to the little black coupe I drove. Once she's settled in the passenger seat, I circle around, turn on the car, and crank the heat.

"Where are you taking me?" she asks finally. In the glow of the car's dashboard, a few specks of blood stand out on her skin.

"Somewhere safe. Don't worry." I put the car in drive and pull out into the constant traffic of the city that never sleeps. "I just have to make a stop first."

10

EYE OF THE STORM

Eleni

I STARE BLANKLY out the window of the sports car Dante poured me into, watching the city whip by. If Dante wanted to kill me, he would have by now, right? He wouldn't bother taking me to a secondary location. My body would blend in with the others covering the floor of the auto shop he whisked me out of. Anyway, he was right. He bought me at the auction. I belong to him. I knew I should never have left without paying my debts.

The gory images I saw on our way out whisk through my mind. The scent of blood teases my nostrils. I know I should feel bad about what I did to Frank, but when I think about the blood, I can only think about Baba, his pained scream. And I can't really think about any of it. So, I stare out the window.

We pause at a stoplight, and I look at Dante. The corners of his mouth pull down, and there's a wrinkle between his dark eyebrows. But he doesn't look upset or worried. Just...focused.

"Are you all right?" My voice rasps out of my throat like I've never used it before.

"Yes," he says slowly. "Why wouldn't I be?"

I blink. "You just shot someone in the face."

A brief, stunned silence passes between us. He meets my gaze in the rearview mirror, his eyes dark and intense.

"You realize what I am, right?"

I shrug vaguely. The gesture reminds me that my head is swimming, that my wrists ache. I just want to go to bed and wake up yesterday.

"Trust me, El, I've done far worse." He turns back to the road.

Somehow, that doesn't make me more comfortable. After a few more turns, he parks the car, then reaches across my lap and opens the glovebox. His forearm brushes my thigh but he doesn't seem to notice, or care, as he grabs an envelope from the glovebox and shuts it with a snap. Without a word, he gets out of the car, crosses in front of it, and opens my door. "This'll be quick."

"I don't want to get out."

He shrugs, the corners of his mouth kicking up with amusement. "I don't know how long this will take, El. I'm not going to waste fuel and risk my favorite car getting stolen by leaving it running."

I look down at my blood splattered pajamas and peer up at him through my lashes. He smirks, shrugging out of his jacket and tosses it in my lap before reaching over me again, unbuckling my seatbelt, and hauling me to my feet.

A single flickering street light illuminates the alley.

I skitter back a step, my heart pounding as I clutch his jacket to my chest. "I'm not going down there. I've seen movies."

He sighs. "There's a bar down there. Benny's. The only entrance is in the alley, and I have some business to take care of. Put the jacket on, your teeth are chattering."

The word "business" turns my stomach. I can't take any more blood.

Somehow, he seems to see that in my face. He withdraws his blood-splattered gun from its holster, puts it in the glovebox, and locks the car while I slide my arms into his jacket. Then, he holds his hand out to me. Just like in the auto shop, I take it. I don't know why.

His palm is warm, and his long, thin fingers slot neatly between mine. But back at Lombardi's, his hand was all I had to hold onto in the darkness. There's something soothing in having that anchor, even when I don't need it.

I follow him into the alley and, as promised, into a dingy little bar. The bartender nods as we walk in.

"Long time, no see." The muscular redhead grabs a tumbler off a rack of cups and sets it on the bar. "Business or pleasure?"

"Little of both, Teo." Dante saunters up to the bar.

I drift behind him.

"None for me, but get our friend here some of Benny's famous fries, and whatever she wants to drink." Dante squeezes my hand and ushers me onto a cracked barstool.

I sit. What else am I going to do? Maybe there's something wrong with me. Maybe I'm in shock. Dante releases my hand, ducks under the bar, and disappears through a beaded curtain.

The bartender, Teo, leans on the bar with a smile. "What do you drink?"

I don't. "Martinis?"

He chuckles. "A woman after my own heart. Nothing quite like a martini when it gets so late it's early again."

I don't tell him that was the only drink I could think of, or that I ordered so no one would be mad. He does the whole routine with the shaker, then pours something clear into a tall, triangular glass and garnishes it with a single olive. The stupid garnish brings tears to my eyes. Baba is dead. Christos is probably dead, even if he was just missing for a while. Mama is missing. I'm the last of the Calimeris family.

When Teo brings out the fries, I eat them automatically. They're hot, crispy, and salty. I barely notice. I could run away, could disappear into the city. Teo looks strong, but I'm faster. The martini starts to disappear, but I'm smart enough to shake my head when he offers me a top off. The bar is already starting to lose definition around the edges, but at least my pain has as well.

I lean on the bar. "Have you ever been kidnapped?"

Teo's eyebrows shoot up. "Can't say that I have. What about you?"

"Pfft." I wave his question away. "You're the weirdo if you haven't. Don't worry about me. I'm fine."

Teo nods slowly. "For sure. Do I need to call someone?"

I laugh until the edges of my laughter grow ragged with tears. "Who would you call?"

Dante steps out of the back room, looks at me, looks at Teo, and communicates something with a gesture I don't understand. Teo takes away my French fries, and I start to object before I see him putting them into a to-go box.

"Will you tell me where we're going now?" I ask Dante as he ducks underneath the bar again.

"I'll tell you I should've ordered you more than fries." He slides his arm under mine. "I take it you don't usually drink anything, not just scotch."

I shake my head. "I've never finished a drink before."

He smiles. "You haven't finished this one."

I glance around for my glass to prove him wrong, but Teo whisks it away and hands Dante the box of fries. With his arm around my shoulders, Dante leads me up the couple stairs, back out to the street. I step on something crunchy, and abruptly, I realize I'm barefoot. I'm still in my pajamas. I don't know if I even own shoes anymore. I know just enough about the mafia to know Frank might have burned down the restaurant just to add insult to injury.

The thought knocks the alcohol instantly out of me. I pry myself away from Dante. I know just enough about the mafia to know a well-meaning boss is a trap, too.

He looks at me for a moment, then just waves me ahead of him. I climb back into the passenger seat because I think Dante could catch me. When he takes the driver's seat and hands me the fries, I look at him.

"Is this the part where you kill me?" I ask. "I'm getting tired of waiting to find out."

He pulls out into traffic with a small smile on his lips. "Your mother wouldn't think much of my manners if I arrived home with your dead body."

My heartbeat roars in my ears. He's a boss. I should've seen this coming. He's taunting me. "I'm exhausted. Please, stop teasing."

"I'm not." His smile grows, and so does my worry. "I'm making an okay impression on your mom right now, and I'd like to keep that going."

Something like hope blossoms in my chest. "Making? In the present?"

"Yes." He turns sharply. "Because she's safe at my house."

My heart hammers. The French fries and the martini threaten to reappear as a riot of emotion tears through me. Mama is alive? I'm not alone in this world?

"Why are you helping me?" I manage to ask.

He smirks. "I had nothing else to do tonight."

I sink back into my seat as the struts and supports of the Verrazano Bridge to Staten Island rise above the skyline.

11

—

REUNION

Eleni

WE PULL up to a gated neighborhood—a tall gate, but not one that looks particularly sturdy or difficult to climb, and Dante waves a plastic card at a man sitting in a booth outside. The man smiles and presses a button to open the gate. I expected Dante to have security, but I didn't expect his security to look like a rent-a-cop. I frown as he drives inside.

The houses past the gate shock me even further. They're bigger than the apartment Mama, Baba, Christos, and I shared, bigger than anything I've seen in the city, but they still look…normal. Two stories. A few big, dramatic windows here and there, but only on a few of the houses. Sizable yards, but not big enough for anything more than a nice patio and a swing set. And there are more houses than I thought, too. A couple dozen, all sharing the security that I assumed Dante needed for himself.

When he pulls up to a completely normal house at the end of one of several cul-de-sacs, my mouth falls open. He's a boss, right? Why

45

does he live in a house that looks like somebody plucked it out of New Jersey?

He takes one look at me and chuckles. "Not impressed?"

I shut my mouth and shake my head. "No, no."

"Don't worry." He climbs out of the car and circles around to open my door before I can. "I like being underestimated."

Since he just said he wasn't going to kill me, and that he saved Mama, I swallow down a comment about how much I doubt anybody has ever underestimated a man who looks like him. He leads me along the curved stone driveway, up a few matching steps, and opens the slate blue front door.

"Zouzouni!" Mama shrieks as she barrels into me.

I wrap my arms around her and stumble back a step, but I can't think about falling, or about how much colliding with her makes my head hurt. She's alive. She's here, and real, and breathing in my arms. I burst into tears and clutch her tighter, inhaling the scent of her night cream, still lingering on her skin.

"I hate to break this up," Dante says, "but is there any chance I could convince you to step inside? I fear the neighbors may have questions soon."

I release Mama with a nod and try to swipe at my tears. She's less interested in taking Dante's orders. She clings to my hand, and I have to drag her inside. At this distance, I can finally actually see her. She's still wearing the nightgown and pants I last saw her in, though someone seems to have given her a sweatshirt as well. Dark bags sag under her eyes, but I don't see any injuries on her.

"Oh." She cups my battered face, and I try not to flinch as she presses on a bruise. "What did they do to you?"

I pat her hand despite the pain. "Don't worry, Mama. Frank's dead."

"What?" Wide-eyed, she looks from me to Dante, who nods.

She doesn't release my hand, but she flings her free arm around him, blabbering thanks in English and Greek. I stand a bit apart from the hug. Why is she thanking him? She knows he's a boss. She knows what involvement with him means.

"It was, ah, nothing." Dante carefully disentangles himself from her embrace. "Can I show you the kitchen? I have a bit of business to take care of, but I don't want to leave you hungry."

My stomach gurgles around the handful of French fries and martini. "Food sounds good."

Mama nods and follows after him like a duckling, though she looks back at me every few seconds, like she's worried I'm going to disappear if she doesn't check often enough. Every time, I smile, though it makes my cheeks ache. Mama is alive.

Dante stops in a bright white kitchen. I blink in the glare.

"I'm not much of a chef, but I'm sure we have most of the basics." He gestures around. "Please, make yourselves at home." And with that, he leaves.

Mama takes his words to heart and finally releases me to bustle around the kitchen. This, at least, looks like someone with mafia money owns it. While the design and size isn't exceptional, I start racking up dollar signs as I look from one state-of-the-art piece of equipment to the next. Years overhearing Mama and Baba complaining about the price of replacing the fryer or the grill top mean I know exactly what not-much-of-a-chef Dante paid for this. But I'm being ridiculous. I have Mama back. I take a seat at the island —in front of a stretch of nearly pure-white marble, not the inset butcher block, and look at her. Somehow, she's already laid out most of the ingredients for *kolokithokeftedes*, zucchini balls, as well as one white onion.

"What happened, Mama?" I ask. "How did you get here?"

She inhales shakily and slices into the white onion. "Let me fix you up first."

Five minutes later, my face is covered with the thin slices of onion Mama swears work more miracles on bruises than any chemical sold in a store, and the tears in my eyes are finally caused by something other than the day I've had. She looks me over once and nods, satisfied.

"Now, will you tell me?" I grab one of the slices before it slides off.

She begins grating zucchini. "Last night, Frank and his men came to the restaurant. He said Baba needed to pay double the usual rate, but he was willing to make a trade." Tears welled in her eyes. "He said—"

I put my hand on her wrist. "I know, Mama. I overheard you talking. And…Frank had me. He made me a similar offer."

Mama's tears disappear as rage lights her face. "It's good that man is dead. No justice in this world with him in it."

I blink. I've never heard Mama talk about anyone like that.

She shakes her head. "He gave us until dawn to decide, though your Baba told him no right away. Clearly, he did not wait for a further answer."

I swallow down my own rage. Baba was killed for an answer that monster already had. Because Frank couldn't wait a few hours for the money I'd almost sold my body for.

"After they…took you, I tried to chase the car." Mama gathers the grated zucchini in cheesecloth and wrings it out, then sets it aside and begins cutting green onions. "Silly, I know, but I couldn't just let him take you. When I couldn't catch up, I went to"—she drops her voice to a whisper—"the *bátsoi*."

The police. I grimace. Mama is right to whisper that word in this house. "And?"

"And nothing. They sent me away. Very strange." She beat together eggs and crumbled feta in a bowl. "I had nothing else to do, so I went back to the restaurant. To be with him." She sniffles.

I grab her hand. "I'm so sorry, Mama."

She shakes her head. "It's better than a mystery we spend the rest of our lives chasing. Dante found me there and brought me here." She glances around as she shakes salt and pepper into the batter. "Do you know why he is helping us?"

My face heats. Mama lost Baba today. I can't tell her what I did.

Can I? The fifty thousand dollars stashed in our apartment might be what we need to get out of here. For good.

"I—"

Dante steps into the kitchen. "Eleni, can you come with me?"

12

PRISON IN THE SKY

Eleni

I RIP ALL the slices of onion off my face while looking at Mama.

"Go," she says, impressing on me with her eyes that I'm not to make the boss whose house we're standing in upset. "I'll get the 'zucchini balls' finished for you."

I stand and join Dante in the doorway. He immediately steps into the hall, then leads me deeper into the house than I've been before. Now, having been in the kitchen, I can see the touches of opulence everywhere. That blue-and-white vase on an end table is probably antique. The plush carpet we pad over is probably from overseas. The leather chair in a nook is probably real.

A door opens ahead of us, and I jump back a step as a beautiful woman in matching leggings and a sports bra steps out. Her long, pitch-black hair curls nearly to her waist, and her dark eyes are emphasized by smoky shadow.

"Oh, sorry." She kisses Dante on the cheek. "I was just headed out."

He nods and doesn't say a word, but I can't resist glancing over my shoulder to watch her disappear out the front door. I shouldn't be surprised Dante has a girlfriend and was going to sleep with me. He's a boss. I have to stop forgetting that.

"We need to talk about what comes next," Dante says as he leads me into a spacious living room.

"Can it be a shower?" I look down at my filthy nightgown.

"Certainly." Dante chuckles as he sits in a deep-red armchair with what seems like the perfect view of the massive TV on the wall. "I could even arrange new clothes, if you like."

I nod, but I don't sit. I don't know what else there is to discuss, other than whether Mama and I are taking the ferry home or not.

Dante sighs. "Look, you and your mother are going to have to stay here for a few days."

"What?" I pale. "Are you kidnapping us?"

"No, no." He holds his hands up. "It's simply that the restaurant—and the apartment above it—are known. And as much as Frank is dead, Luca very much isn't."

I swallow. The money's in the apartment. There's no escape for Mama and me without that money. But I'll be happiest if I never see any Lombardis again.

"Why here?" I ask. "Why are you helping us at all?"

Dante runs a hand through his dark hair and suddenly looks the ten years older than me that I suspect he is. "Frank Lombardi killed my father. Happened about five years back, now. I went to The Greek Corner to rattle his cage a little, and you ended up being a very convenient way to rattle his cage a hell of a lot more." He shakes his head. "But that's not the point. I need to know why Frank took you instead of killing you."

I cross my arms—how dare he talk about me like nothing more than a pawn in his game—but my fickle heart aches. I want to ask how it happened, if he found his father like I found Baba, if he knows how long I'll keep smelling Baba's blood every time I turn. For a brief moment, I'm grateful to that monster Leo for putting the bag over my head before he dragged me into the living room. I don't want those images in my mind.

"He wants—wanted me for Luca." I swallow. "As a bride. He

made the offer to Baba first and killed him because he said no." I scrub my hands over my arms and wish he'd let me shower first. "When Frank made the offer to me, he said my options were Luca or the rest of his men. And he said Luca had bad taste, or something."

I can't help it. I glance at Dante to see his reaction. He went to the virginity auction, so clearly a woman being pure is important to him.

I don't expect to see his face turn into a thundercloud. Powerful rage, just as deep as I saw from Mama in the kitchen, mars his features. But only for a split second. He blinks, and it's gone, leaving him nothing more than the smooth-faced don of the Staten Island Saints once more.

"I'll handle it," he says. "You just stay here with your…mama. Don't worry."

I take a step closer to him. "Whatever Luca wants with me has nothing to do with your dad."

He sucks in a deep breath and exhales slowly. "What makes you say that?"

"I was there." I hug my arms tighter around myself. "He didn't say anything about you or your dad. Why do you care what he wanted with me?"

Dante looks at me for a long moment, scanning me from head to toe. I've been with him for hours now, it seems, and I suddenly feel underdressed. That liquid heat returns to his gaze, but it's muddied by a dozen other emotions I can't pull apart.

"You shouldn't have been swept up in this in the first place," he says.

I take a step back like I've been hit. Another rejection. He doesn't want me for anything specific. Not anymore.

"That's big talk from the man who pulled me into it," I say. "You used me to get at Frank. You said it yourself."

He stands. "That's not what I—"

"No." I take another step closer. "You asked if I knew what you are? Well, I do. You're a mafia boss, and that means I can't trust a word you say. Every gift you give comes with strings. If you really want me to stop worrying, you'll let me leave, because I couldn't ever relax here."

His dark eyes are intense, burning. "El—"

"Don't use nicknames for me." I whirl away. I can't get distracted. "I won't forget what you are again. I bet that's why you bought me at the auction in the first place, because you saw me, and you recognized an in."

"I would've bought you no matter what," Dante murmurs as he strides out of the living room past me. "And this wasn't a discussion. Take whichever of the bedrooms upstairs you want, and shower at your leisure." He turns back and meets my gaze. "Do anything you like. Just don't go open the last door to the left upstairs. That's my room."

"Fine," I bite out, but he's already gone.

I follow the smell of frying oil back to Mama.

13

BREADCRUMBS

Dante

I step into the basement beneath Piacere and shut the door behind me. Flickering fluorescents light the racks and racks of liquor, spare stool, and coils of velvet rope. To the unknowing eye, the perfectly legal basement of a perfectly legal club owner. I snort and head for the third alcohol shelf from the left on the far wall, then rap on the metal I can just reach through the glimmering glass bottlenecks. After a brief pause, the whole section of wall swings aside, and I cross into the real basement.

Here, the lights are brilliant and steady. Only the best for my men. Clean, crisp metal lines the walls and the floor. Easy to clean. Hard to escape quietly over. Tony pushes the button to send the decoy rack careening back into place.

"Took you long enough." He wipes the back of his hand over his forehead, and I see blood over his fingernails. "Not that the bastard's broken yet."

I nod. My shoes click against the floor as we stride to the corner of the basement where the capo he pulled out of the auto shop before they wrecked it waits. We need to take the Lombardi family out once and for all, and that means finding a way to Luca.

The capo lolls in a metal chair, with his arms and legs bound to different parts of the seat. Blood streams from a cut on his forehead and bruises purple his bare chest, but he smirks at me as I walk up.

"So, I rate the big guns?" he says. "Interesting."

"Is it?" I grab a meat tenderizing mallet and test its weight, then pull the capos hand onto a low table. "Interesting to who, Luca? Is he the heir?"

The capo shakes his head. "I'm not telling you shit."

I sigh and glance at Tony, who shrugs. I bring the meat mallet down on the capo's index finger with a crack. He barely smothers his scream.

"Not bad." I nod. "I see Frank trains his men to endure pain. But rest assured, Frank didn't have enough brains in his thick fucking skull to come up with the kinds of torture I can. We're just getting started. You want to tell me about the lines of succession now?"

The capo hisses out a breath between his teeth and says nothing. I crush another finger without waiting, and this time, he yelps.

"Getting there." I roll my eyes at Tony. "Almost a word. Do we want to try something easier? How about your name?"

"Leo," he grunts.

"Leo, good." I smile as Tony circles around behind him, and Leo twists in his seat, trying to see my capo. "Well, Leo, who inherits the Lombardi farm?"

There's a pause. I crush two more fingers and grab his thumb.

"Gotta be faster than that, Leo." I chuckle. "Just one left. But I'm getting tired of the mallet. Tony, can you grab me the pliers?"

Leo goes white.

"Yeah, I think I'll take the fingernail." I lean my weight on his broken pinkie as I twist his thumb painfully back.

Leo chokes on a scream.

"I've got a bit of a collection," I lie. "You'll be surprised how badly it hurts."

"Fuck!" Leo squirms. "What do you wanna know? You want to

know about those fucking Greeks we just dropped?"

I grin at Tony, who hasn't moved. Tony frowns back at me. He doesn't care.

"What do you know about Frank's dealings with the Calimeris family?" I grab a knife off a nearby table and twirl it between my fingers.

A bead of sweat drips into Leo's eyes. "Frank's been obsessed with their daughter for going on two years now. Offered a bunch to the family to take her off their hands, but they fucking refused." He starts to laugh, but it turns into a cough as I slam the hilt of the knife into his chest.

"What?" he gasps. "I'm telling the truth."

"Tell it without the color commentary," I hiss.

"Color commentary or no story." He smirks as if he's got the upper hand.

I spin the knife in my grip and trace the point over his skin.

"Fuck, fine." He shakes his head as if to clear it. "Frank's been yammering on about giving her to Luca, and he finally put the screws to the dad. Doubles the fee, says he's collecting early, the whole nine. Dickhead wouldn't cave, so Frank sent a guy in to explain what happens to people who deny Frank, and put me on delivery duty."

Ice seeps through my veins. I'm looking into the smiling, bloody face of the man who'd kidnapped Eleni from her childhood home. To hear him tell it, he hadn't touched her dad, but I didn't believe this sniveling sack of shit any more than I was going to let him see the light of day again.

"Oh yeah," he says. "I carried the little Greek slut out. Have you slapped her ass yet? It's—"

I withdraw my gun and fire a single bullet directly between his eyebrows.

"What the fuck?" Tony demands. "Even I didn't think he was done yet, and you're usually the last one hanging on."

I blink. A little of the white-hot, all-consuming rage that came over me when Leo called Eleni a slut starts to ebb. Tony's right. He might've had more.

Still, I clean any residue off my palms with a handkerchief and tuck my gun away. "I was done with him. Clearly, he was just trying to piss us off."

"Yeah, it's a good thing you stay so calm." Tony shakes his head at the corpse. "Well, shit. Seems like a safe bet that Luca's slated for the top spot."

I nod, and we start to walk out together. The cleaning crew will deal with Leo's body.

"If that's true, then that Eleni girl is still in the middle of this." Tony huffs a breath. "That is, if Frank told his son about his chosen bride."

The word bride makes me start to see red again. I shake my head to clear it. I'm the boss of the goddamn Staten Island Saints, not some kid sticking up a gas station with a BB gun, and I have to act like it.

"She's in the middle of this no matter what," I reply.

Tony frowns at me.

For the first time, I don't know how to explain what I'm thinking. All I know is that I've seen something in her. I saw a flicker of it at the virginity auction, the determination that infused her when she refused me, when she decided to sleep with me. I saw it when she told me to kill Frank without flinching. And I saw a little of it at my house earlier, when she told me she wasn't staying. Eleni might dress like a nun and act like the girl next door, but she's got some backbone under all that. There's a fire in her. One I want to stick my hand in just to see what burns.

But if I can't do that—and I very much can't, with the mess she's at the center of—I want to let it loose and see what happens. She won't be satisfied with Frank's death. It was too quick, too easy. She'll want more revenge. And that means she might be willing to play the game. If she's as tough as I think she is, we might be able to take out every sprig of the Lombardi tree. I smile. If I can get Thano on board, we can even split the city between ourselves.

"Hey." Tony nudges me. "What the fuck are you thinking? What are you going to do about Eleni and her mom?"

"That"—I face Tony with a wide grin—"depends on Eleni."

14

LATE NIGHT SNACK

Eleni

I ROLL over and tug on the heavy blankets covering the king bed Mama and I decided to share. They don't move, and Mama's light snores issue through the darkness. She's finally fallen asleep. Part of me is thankful, and the rest wishes I had enough blankets to cover myself. As soon as she finished the zucchini balls, she collapsed into one of the tall seats at the kitchen island, weeping. I've been at her side, holding her and offering her toilet paper because I couldn't find tissues, since. Exhaustion still drags off my limbs, reminding me that I haven't really gotten a good night's sleep since the night before the auction, but I can't sleep. I just keep thinking of the smell of blood, and the stories about Baba Mama kept trying to tell through her tears.

With a sigh, I push the covers off and climb out of bed. I didn't take Dante up on his offer of new clothes, but two new nightgowns appeared on the end of the bed between when Mama and I picked it, and when we finally decided to crawl into bed. The fine, white fabric clings to me in a way my old one didn't, and despite the underwear I still have on underneath, I feel more naked than I was before. Still, if the clock on the wall is right, it's nearly three in the morning. No one will see me.

My stomach growls, a reminder Mama's sudden breakdown kept me from eating any of the zucchini balls, and I creep back downstairs to the kitchen.

As expected, the house is dark and still, so the light when I open the refrigerator is blinding. I cover my eyes and grab for the container I very awkwardly asked one of the maids milling around for when it became clear Mama wouldn't be eating any time soon.

A door slides open behind me, and I whirl with the container in hand. Stepping in through a sliding glass door in the breakfast nook past the kitchen is the beautiful woman I saw earlier. Dante's girl-friend. She's still wearing the same leggings and sports bra, but glitter coats her from head to toe. I slam the fridge door.

"Don't worry, you're not in trouble." She holds her hands up with a smile. "Dante's got enough money that none of us need to worry about food."

"Right." I set the container down on the counter anyway, suddenly no longer hungry. I have no idea what the etiquette is for meeting mafia girlfriends in the dead of night in their own kitchen. "Um, thank you so much for letting us stay in your house."

"My—?" Her eyebrows shoot up. "Yeah, I don't own any of this. Everything the refrigerator light touches is Dante's."

I nod. "Sorry, I just assumed, since you're together—"

She bursts into laughter, and I stop dead. Panic warms my face. Why is this funny?

After a long moment, she wipes away a tear. "Sorry. Dante would be so lucky to date someone like me. No, I don't even live here."

"Oh." I glance at her out of the corner of my eye. She's obviously gorgeous, skinny with curves in all the right places, and tall enough to actually look good with them. If Dante's not dating her right now, I'm certain he wants to be. Every man would.

"I've completely blown this." She sticks her hand out, and I notice a duffel bag over her shoulder. "I'm Gianna. Dante asked me to stay here for a couple of days so you and your mom wouldn't be alone."

I shake her hand carefully. "Mama's asleep."

"I'm wiped anyway." She scrubs a hand over her makeup. "Long night. Any chance I could grab one of those for the road?"

I open the container and offer her a zucchini ball. Despite what she said, she bites into it immediately, and moans at the flavor. A small, proud smile crosses my face. Even on the worst day of her life, Mama's a better chef than almost everyone I've ever met.

"These are incredible," she mumbles through a full mouth. "Do you guys want to stay at my place next?"

I almost laugh at that. It's easier to like Gianna when she's complimenting Mama. "Long night doing what, if I could ask?"

"Oh!" She stuffs the rest of the ball into her mouth and chews quickly. "Damn, Dante really didn't explain anything. I dance at Piacere."

My face flames as I remember the scantily clad women I saw on the poles. "That's very…impressive."

She laughs. "It is. I can teach you someday, if you want. But it means if I stay standing for another minute, I'm gonna collapse." She grabs a few more zucchini balls and waves over her shoulder as she heads for the same door I saw her coming out of earlier.

Despite how pleasantly the interaction ended, I can't stomach the idea of food anymore. I close up the zucchini balls and put them away, then trudge back up the stairs. Gianna seems…well, okay, she seems very nice. But I can't shake the tightness in my chest when I picture her. And her offer to teach me to dance like she does is sweet, but I'll never be able to move like her. I'll just look silly or slutty, not sexy like I bet she does. I don't even blame Dante for wanting to date her.

At the top of the stairs, I turn left. Mama will be so upset if she wakes up and I'm not in bed with her. I never should've gone to get a snack. I didn't even eat anything.

I arrive at the end of the hall and wince. Mama and I took a bedroom on the right. I'm not used to a house with so many lefts and rights to keep track of. But as I start to turn back, I realize the door is slightly ajar.

The door at the end of the hall to the left. Dante's bedroom.

I can just barely hear Gianna singing something off-key downstairs. Mama is still asleep, or she'd be yelling. And Dante left hours ago. A small peek can't hurt.

I step inside and peer around the massive bedroom. Part of me expects it to be all dark reds, like Piacere, and that part is disappointed. The walls are a deep, dusty blue, and the huge bed in the middle has a simple gray comforter. I take a few steps closer and touch the mattress. Another surprise. The intense boss sleeps in plush comfort, not a hard board to keep him sharp. The soft leather shackles on the four posters of the frame turn my stomach, and I pray everyone he's had in those agreed to be there.

When I turn away, I know I should leave, but my eye catches on a wall of pictures. Dozens, hundreds of them, all featuring a smiling Dante and some number of other people. I drift over to study it and suddenly remember the wrinkles around his mouth. I thought he looked like he smiled more than he frowned, and this display is proof.

One picture catches my attention, and my heart skips a beat. I pull it off the wall and peer closer. I have to be wrong. But no, I'm looking at a full-color picture of my brother Christos with his arm around Dante, both of them smiling like they've never had a care.

Mama and I have to leave. Now. No matter what Dante says. I turn to go get her.

Just in time to see Dante stepping into the room.

"I thought I told you not to come in here." He locks the door behind him.

15

———

COMARE

Eleni

MY STOMACH DROPS to my toes. Dante prowls away from the door toward me. I've really messed up now.

"Do you always break the rules laid out for you?" he asks.

I swallow. There's a growl in his voice, but it doesn't sound angry. It tingles down my spine and warms something in my gut. I'm suddenly very aware that I'm in a nightgown again, and while this one is soft, it is nearly as thick as my old one.

"Not until recently," I manage.

Something lights in his eyes. "You know, there are punishments for disobeying me in my house."

He is a boss. I should be dropping everything in my hands and sprinting away. My heart pounds in that same place in my gut.

I take a step closer to him with my chin high. "What kind of punishment can I expect then?"

His eyes flame. He's only a few inches away now, so close that I could reach out and grab him if I wanted to. I could pull him in. But the air between us feels thick, impassable.

"What's in your hand?" he asks.

I jar back into myself. What am I thinking? I don't know him, I can't trust him. By just stepping into the room, he made me completely forget what I was holding in the first place. I glance down and find the picture of him with Christos. Right. Baba believes— believed Luca killed Christos, and so do I. But with this picture in my hand, with the way he always seems to cloud my mind, it's difficult to deny that Dante could've done it just as easily. Wordlessly, I hand the photo to him.

He takes it and steps back. "Christos. I should've known you'd beeline for this."

"How did you—" I can't quite make the words come out. Dante seems to understand anyway.

"We overlapped at Wagner." He starts walking back over to the wall of photos, seemingly to pin the one I removed back up. "Actually played football together for a couple years there."

Wagner. The college Mama and Baba sent Christos to for four whole years. Even though he only lived on Staten Island, we barely saw him more than weekends. Baba said Christos needed a business degree to take over The Greek Corner one day, and Wagner was the closest place where Christos got in. Dimly, I remembered screaming in packed stands at a few of his football games. Had I heard the name Cattaneo? I didn't know anymore.

"Oh," I say as he pins it back in place. "W-why did you stop?"

He smiles. "The family business needed me."

I nod. He knew Christos years before he disappeared. There's no way. But the question bubbles to my lips and—

"Do you know what happened to him?" I blurt.

Dante stares at the floor. "I didn't even know he had a little sister back then. He was just Freshman Chris, this genius running back I was waiting to see pop up in the NFL someday."

I hear the no without him having to say it. But something about the way he avoids the word drives me across the floor toward him. He didn't say never, or absolutely not. He didn't say anything.

"Could you find out?" I ask. "We haven't heard anything in two years."

He takes a step back. "I don't know. You're asking me to overturn old dirt, make a mess all over again."

I'm not stupid. I've overheard Baba talking to Frank enough times. Dante is bargaining. He won't do this for free, wants to know what I'm willing to offer. I swallow, and that heat in my gut kicks up again. I've seen the way he looks at me. I might just be a waitress with a quarter of a nighttime computer science degree, but I know I have something he wants.

"I'll do anything," I say, trying to drop my voice lower like he did before. "I can clean, or be bait, or be your...*comare*." The Italian word rolls awkwardly off my Greek tongue.

He stops stepping back. "Why would you think I want a mistress?"

"Uh." I blink, startled. Have I read this wrong? "I was just thinking that you bought me at the auction, so—"

"The auction." He takes a step closer to me. "What about that made you think I was in need of a mistress instead of just a good time?"

The words good time shiver down my spine. "It wasn't the auction. I actually met your girlfriend downstairs, and—"

He raises an eyebrow. He's back within grabbing distance. I feel so lost in this conversation that I don't even consider it this time.

Well, not really.

"Yeah, um"—I cast through my scrambled memory for her name—"Gianna?"

Like she did when I suggested them together, Dante laughs. "Gianna is my cousin. I just asked her to stay here for a few days, for you and your mom's sake."

Cousin. Her laughter. He'd be so lucky to date someone like her. That was what she meant.

"So, you just went to the auction for a good time," I mumble, only half aware I'm speaking aloud.

Dante circles behind me, like a shark waiting for a boat to tip, and I shiver. Somehow, losing the ability to look into his night-dark eyes feels more dangerous than showing him my unprotected back. Am I about to experience one of the punishments he was talking about?

"Why do you keep bringing up the auction?" he asks.

"I...didn't..." But of course, I did. I keep thinking about the favor he said I owed him instead of my body, how high my tab must be now. I simply don't want to be in his debt.

Dante hums as he circles back around to where I can see him, and my heart skips a beat as I realize he has loosened his black tie to reveal a small triangle of skin at his throat. The room feels small and close. Is there enough space to breathe without touching him? Was there ever?

"You keep saying I bought you," he murmurs. "I can't help wondering why you're thinking about it."

"I owe you," I manage.

The smile that pulls his lips is all hunger. "You're trembling. Your pupils are dilated, and that long nightgown of yours hides a lot, but it doesn't hide how fast you're breathing."

My breath races in my ears, harsh and wanting. But what do I want?

Dante leans in. "Does the feeling of being owned turn your blood molten?"

I don't nod. I think.

His breath whispers over the shell of my ear, so hot it lights that place in my gut aflame. Whatever he says next, I'll agree with. He's a boss. I'm in more danger than I've ever experienced in my life. Baba was murdered yesterday, and Mama's asleep in the other room. But I am melting under waves of Dante's heat.

"Then go to sleep," he says.

Before I can think twice, he leans back and saunters toward what seems to be a closet on the other side of the room.

"What?" I say.

"You heard me," he replies. "If you want me to be in charge, go the fuck to bed. It's the middle of the night, and I doubt you've slept well these last couple days."

I haven't, but I'm still burning up. The only word in my mind is want. I want nothing more than to climb into his bed, to pay off what I owe him, to let him own me for the night.

He slides his tie out of his collar without looking at me. The message is clear. He's going to bed alone.

I unlock the door and stumble out of his room on strangely wobbly legs. Mama needs me. But that thing in my gut that only wanted to stay back in Dante's room with him still burns through me, leaving me confused and disappointed.

DECISION TIME

Eleni

I WAKE SLOWLY the next morning and yawn. I can't hear Mama and Baba in the kitchen, so I've slept in a little, but there's not enough sun filtering in through my closed eyelids to be truly that late in the day. Exhaustion clings to my limbs like I stayed up all night finishing a paper, but the tables won't wait themselves. I open my eyes and sit up.

My heart slams the brakes. I'm in a huge bed in an even bigger room decorated in simple, neutral tans. Where are the soft blue walls I picked out when we were redoing the restaurant, and Baba found a buy-one-get-one sale on paint? Where is the creaky twin bed I've slept in my whole life? Where are Mama and Baba?

At the thought of them, memories start to filter back in. The auction. Sneaking home with enough money to save our lives. Baba's heavy expression as he carried the baseball bat to the door. The smell of Baba's blood–and Frank and all those strange men on the floor of the auto shop. And Dante, in the corner of every memory. I'm in his house. And I can't leave.

I suck in a deep breath and climb out of bed. In the attached bathroom, I find a steam-covered mirror with a note from Mama.

Went to make breakfast. Sleep in.

I shake my head. Dante will have to start buying more groceries if Mama's going to cook like this. But even that feels strange to think about. How can I care about groceries when Baba's gone? What more is there?

In the closet, I find a single set of clothes, which looks like an unbranded version of the uniform Mama and Baba had me wear at The Greek Corner, except for the apron. Dante has only seen me in that and the funeral dress. As I pull the loose shirt and skirt on, I thank whoever might be listening that he didn't choose the funeral dress instead. Then, I brush my teeth with a packaged toothbrush sitting on the counter and head downstairs.

Mama sits at the kitchen island like she can't bring herself to move to the small table a few feet away, halfway through her usual breakfast of toast with butter and honey, a boiled egg, orange juice, and coffee so black it gives Dante's eyes a run for their money. The smells remind me so much of home I start to tear up.

"Zouzouni," she says. "I boiled an egg for you, if you want it."

I take the egg out of the ice bath for something to do with my hands. I'm too nauseous to eat. "How did you sleep, Mama?"

She smiles wanly. "You know most of it. But what about you? I am sorry I put so much on you yesterday. I'm better now."

I look her over and immediately see the lie in her words. Her hair is wet but somehow already askew, and the clothes Dante bought for her fit obviously less well than mine. All of her cuticles are red with blood, and none of her expressions reach her eyes. Still, I know what she means. She means she intends to be the mom again, instead of letting me fix things.

"I'm okay," I lie. This time, I know better than Mama does. I can fix things. "I was kind of in and out too."

She nods. I peel the egg carefully, trying to keep the shell connected as much as I can.

"I was thinking," Mama says.

I turn to her. I know her serious voice.

"What if, once Dante is satisfied we won't be gunned down for stepping outside, you and I head back to Parikia?" She glances at me. "Theía Adriani just had your second cousin. She offered to chip in for the tickets if we help out around the house a little."

I blow out a long breath. Mama has a complicated relationship with her younger sister, mostly because Theía Adriani thinks Mama ran away to chase her dreams. If she's willing to move in with her, Mama must be serious.

"Can we afford it?" I ask, thinking of the money I stashed in the apartment before I was kidnapped. If Dante met Mama there, surely Frank's men didn't have time to comb the whole place.

"I think so," she says shakily. "Especially if I—" She swallows and spins her wedding ring around her finger.

My heart leaps into my throat. Mama's wedding ring was a present from Baba on their tenth anniversary, a little joke between them because they'd gotten married on the way to the boat for America, so neither of them had rings for years. She cried when she opened the ring, and he said he finally had the money to make her shine like she deserved. She doesn't have a more treasured possession.

"No, Mama," I say quickly. "We can figure it out without that."

"We?" She meets my gaze. "I was worried you might fight me, zouzouni."

I swallow. Six months ago, I started my night classes. I told my parents it was because I had so much fun redoing the website, and that was what helped me pick my major, but the truth was that I decided to go to school because of another run- in with Frank's men.

They caught me on the restaurant floor alone, grabbed me, but Mama came down before anything terrible happened. She couldn't do anything but turn bright red. Later that night, I heard her crying to Baba about how she felt like she betrayed me. That was the first moment I felt a flicker of the anger that had driven me over these last few days, and I knew. I had to get myself and my family out of the mafia. And this is my chance to do exactly that.

But something about this situation makes me want to wait and see. Frank's blood doesn't smell as stomach-churning in my memory as the rest of it. I don't want to walk away from the ground the men who killed Baba and Christos still walk.

When I think about it like that, the fire lights in me again. Here, in Dante's kitchen, in the light of what only people working in restaurants could call late morning, the flame doesn't just feel like rage. It feels like certainty, like determination. It feels alive, maybe for the first time in my life. Whatever else Dante said last night, he didn't say he wouldn't find answers for Christos.

"I don't know, Mama," I say honestly. "There's so much here—"

She grabs my hand. "There's so much pain, so much violence. I never should've left Greece. Please, come home with me."

I look into her eyes, so like mine, and know that no matter what else happens, Mama can't stay.

"I have to go to the restaurant," I say.

Mama stares blankly at me.

"All our things are there." I shrug. I don't need to tell her that I won't know until I'm standing in the place where I lost Baba whether I can ever really leave.

She doesn't say anything as I set my perfectly peeled egg on the edge of her plate and walk away.

17

TURNING THE CORNER

Eleni

I WANDER THE HALLS, searching for Dante to ask if he'll take me to the restaurant, and nearly run into another tall, suited man. I stumble back a step, and he catches me before I fall.

"Did I put on my invisible suit today?" he asks as he sets me back on my feet.

"What?" He's handsome, in a square way, and he has piercing blue eyes. I know him from somewhere.

"Dante always says I make a bad first impression." He shoves his hands in his pockets. "I'm Tony Bellini, caporegime around here."

The pieces snap into place. He surrounded Frank in the auto shop. But if he's a caporegime, then finding him is almost as good as finding Dante.

"Can you take me into the city?" I ask. "I need to see the restaurant."

"Why?"

I take a deep breath. "I have a decision to make."

Tony shrugs and leads me down a new hall.

I CLIMB out of the black car Tony drove to the restaurant, a sedan so minutely different from Dante's, I wouldn't be able to tell the difference if every detail of my drive with Dante hadn't been inscribed on my memory. Somehow, the restaurant still stands there, just the same as it always did. I watch a cluster of college kids, new to the neighborhood last month, walk up to the door, jingle it a few times, and walk away frowning when they discover it's locked. My heart thuds hollowly.

Tony climbs out. "I gotta go with you."

I nod. I expected that. Once the college kids are gone, I open the door into the restaurant. Police tape covers the tables, their chairs still stacked on top with their legs in the air like they're waiting for a new day that will never come, and the open, empty register. I look at Tony.

"Cops came in, took a few pictures this morning." He shakes his head. "But that'll do as much good as lighting candles, chanting in Latin, and hoping you're secretly a witch. The Lombardis own damn near every cop in the city."

I try to smile at him. I think that was his attempt at lightening the mood, and I suppose it's nice someone's trying. I ignore the bare register—after everything, Frank stole from us?—and pluck the tiny polymer-clay olive off the counter next to it. In sixth grade, Christos was assigned a project in art class to make a piece using any medium that was about family. He'd been in a bad mood that year, so he made a single green olive, stuffed with American pimento, and completely invented a heart-wrenching story to tell the class when his turn came to present. The teacher gave him an A, so Mama stuck it to the counter because her son was an artist. She was so proud.

He only ever told me the whole story. I pocket it before Tony can ask.

In the kitchen, I grab Mama's good apron, Baba's favorite spatula. I can't explain why, but I need them. Then, I glance at Tony.

"Is it okay if I go upstairs?"

He takes one look at my face. "Great timing. I have to make a private call." He lifts his phone to his ear without dialing, and I smile just a little as I climb the back stairs.

When I unlock the door to the apartment, my smile disappears. Baba's blood covers the carpet in huge, dark red patches. The smell rolls out in a wave. I clap a hand to my mouth and run deeper into the apartment, glass I don't remember breaking crunching under my feet. In Mama and Baba's room, I grab the scrapbooks she made when Christos and I were each born and clothes for Mama. I stuff as many clothes as I can fit into my backpack, as well as my scant makeup collection, like that matters. Then, I wobble into the bathroom. Dimly, I realize I've never been inside with shoes on when my heels slide on the toilet lid.

But the money is there. A thick, heavy envelope. Something breaks in my chest, and I sink to the toilet, clutching it to my chest.

I sob.

A few moments later, I hear footsteps crunching over glass. I want to pull myself together, to be ready for what must come next, but the tears won't stop.

Dante steps into the doorway. It's the last thing I expect, and I actually laugh through my tears, conjuring a huge bubble of snot. He'll tell me to leave, but he'll never want me now. Not when he's just seen me so raw, so broken, with my arms full of all my family has left and tears streaming down my cheeks.

He sinks to the ground in the doorway and, like a much younger man, pulls his knees to his chest. He reminds me of Christos in that moment, how he used to watch Saturday morning cartoons far too close to the television. The tears overtake me again, and I momentarily forget a mafia boss is watching me fall apart.

Only when my tears start to dry up do I realize he's still there.

"I'm sorry," he says quietly. "You didn't deserve this."

Ironic, coming from a mafia boss. How many families has he left like this? Does he even care?

But I don't say that. I say, "I actually thought I'd found a way out."

He nods, and I know he realizes I'm talking about the auction.

"But I should've known." I shake my head. "Even then, I couldn't help getting in deeper. And now we've lost everything." My gaze catches on my backpack in the corner, and I suddenly realize that I could've made more space for clothes if I took my textbooks out. A wet laugh bubbles out of my throat. "What am I going to do now, go to class? Take my finals?"

He leans his head back against the door frame. "I didn't know you were in college."

"Night classes." I swipe at my tears as the intensity of emotion starts to ebb. "Computer science."

He nods. "Do you know what you want to do with that?"

"Make the website better?" I shrug. "I don't know. It's not like I was ever going to work anywhere other than here. I just—" I shake my head.

"Just what?" he asks.

There's a real interest in Dante's eyes, like nothing I've ever seen in him before. It pulls a truth I've never spoken aloud from my lips.

"I just like—liked having something that was mine. Programming is quiet. Private." More tears well up. "I love my family, don't misunderstand."

"I don't," he says. "I actually really understand."

I peer at him. His face is relaxed, easy, and I don't know what to make of him.

"Mama wants to go home," I say. "She wants me to go with her."

Dante meets my gaze. "What do you want?"

His dark eyes burn through me and ignite that fire. Everything I've ever had solely for myself started with this flame. And this time, I know exactly what I want.

I want every Lombardi dead for what they did to us.

"Mama will be safe in Greece," I say. "But I'm not going anywhere."

"You want revenge." It's not a question. "I can help you, but you need to know what you're asking for. You'd be part of the mafia, El."

My decision is made. "I'll do whatever it takes."

He hops to his feet with a cocky grin that lights my blood on fire and holds out his hand to help me up. "Welcome to the Saints."

18

MAKING A MAFIOSA

Dante

A FEW DAYS LATER, I stride through the quiet main floor of Piacere a few hours before opening with Tony at my side.

"So, this is it, then," he says. "You've finally lost it."

I chuckle. "I haven't lost it. You're just not seeing the whole picture."

"Oh, okay." He holds his hands up sarcastically. "No, you're right, please tell me what I'm not seeing in plain sight, Dante. Turn a Greek Schoolgirl into a Staten Island Saint? Is she ex-FBI, or a ninja, or?"

I slug him in the arm. "You're a douche. She's something Luca Lombardi wants, something he doesn't know we still have."

Talking about Eleni like this feels wrong, but Tony's been on my ass since I told him in the car on the way back from the restaurant, and I'm tired of having this argument. At least, if he understands her as a chess piece, he'll fucking understand.

"And you want to lure him out." Tony runs his hands over his face, and I see the frustration of the meeting we just left wash over him.

I've had all my top guys on Luca since we dropped Frank, but no one has seen hide nor hair of him in days. Everybody's getting touchy.

"You're playing with fire," he says. "You know that, right?"

"What?" I raise an eyebrow at him. "Two minutes ago, she was a Greek schoolgirl."

"She is, don't get me wrong." Tony holds the door open for me. "But she's also hell bent on revenge. I just worry about that flaming out."

The word flame pulls me inexorably back to that moment in my room, when she lifted her chin at me and asked what kind of punishment she could expect. She'd never recognize it in a million years, but right behind her at that moment was a body-safe candle. My brain has been teasing me with images of wax patterns drawn over her delicate skin, over her impertinent mouth.

"Worry about Luca Lombardi," I say as I step out. "And Thano Coppola. He's a wild card, and I don't want him to think we need him as much as we do." I glance at the sunset sky. "So I want you to take this meeting by yourself."

Tony rolls his eyes and is clearly about to object, but I climb into my car and start heading home before he can. Thano isn't dangerous unless we let him get cocky, and making him think a personal meeting only ranks my caporegime should help with that.

None of which has anything to do with why I'm driving home. So, I spend the whole ride mastering myself once again.

When I walk inside and find Eleni with her mother, I say, "Come with me."

They both rise.

"Just Eleni," I bark sharper than I mean to.

She exchanges a look I pretend not to see with her mother and follows me. She's wearing yet another loose outfit, and I consider asking her to change, but I don't want to say anything about her clothes. That opens a door I need to keep closed. Three days ago, she was weeping in the apartment where her father died and telling me she'd lost everything. Despite what my brain—and my cock—keep suggesting, I need to keep our relationship strictly business.

We climb into the car together, but I avoid her questions until we arrive at the nearest gun range, which agreed to stay open late for me. She stares warily at the building.

"Have you ever shot a gun before?" I ask.

She shakes her head.

"Without that skillset, you're dead." I exit the car and stride inside. She follows, keeping her chin tilted high in a show of bravery, but her eyes are still weary.

What am I doing? Why can't I treat her like I treat any of my men, like a friend or acquaintance or, hell, even a coworker at this point? The ice in my tone toward her feels wrong, all wrong.

The attendant gets her settled with a smaller pistol that fits in her palm and ear protection. I pick up a larger pistol, just in case I need to show her anything, and we enter the empty range. Eleni looks at me, wide-eyed.

"Have you ever even held a gun before?" I ask.

She bites her lip, then shakes her head.

"Okay." I suck in a breath. "Let's start with the basics."

I walk her through keeping the muzzle pointed down, never putting her finger on the trigger unless she's ready to shoot, and other simple gun safety.

"All right, fire one," I say.

"What?" She looks around, lost and panicky and nothing like the burning, confident version of her I've seen before.

Whatever is making me the worst version of myself relents. I nod at one of the lanes. "I'll show you. Just come here."

She does so, holding the gun away from her like it's a snake. I smile.

"First, your grip," I say. "You want to hold it tight. It's gonna kick no matter what, and you're less likely to lose your gun that way."

She raises her right hand and squeezes the butt of the gun. I swallow another smile.

"Both hands, El."

She glances at me and grabs the butt with both hands. If I don't get in there, she's fucked. I set my gun down and step closer, then reposition her hands myself.

"Like this," I murmur. "Thumb on the hammer, index finger right below the trigger."

She's so close I can feel her warmth. Her stance is a wreck. She'll topple over if I let her go. She'll pull her arms back and pistol whip herself the second she fires the gun if I'm not guiding her movements. I can touch her like this, just this once. It means nothing. This is just business. "You'll want to stand to the side." I try not to notice how my breath ghosts over her cheek. "Like this."

I wrap my other hand around her waist and pull until she repositions her hips to match my own. Her whole body lines up with mine, and I smother a groan. I should've taken advantage of the auction when I had a chance. Now, she's a line I can't cross. Even though she sleeps a few rooms away every night, in that fucking nightgown that I swear I can almost see through when the light hits just right.

"Is that good?" she asks breathily.

I glance down at her and realize her eyes have fluttered closed, that she's leaning her weight back against me. My cock reacts. It would be so easy to claim that mouth of hers.

"Perfect." I flatten my hand against her stomach, pulling her even closer.

Her breath catches.

"When you fire," I say. "You need to mean it. Finger on the trigger, roll it back, and know you're taking a life. Know you want to take that life."

She moves her finger to the trigger.

"Fire," I murmur into the shell of her ear.

The sound cracks through the space, startling us both out of whatever spell just fell over us. I pull back and hit the button to bring the target forward.

Eleni is an innocent, someone who would never be in this position if I hadn't intervened. She's been robbed of the life she deserves. And no matter what she thinks, her position in this life is temporary. I'm going to get her out.

The target slides forward to reveal a single, perfect shot to the heart. Eleni squeals and throws her arms around me.

I'll get her out...eventually.

19

WHAT DO YOU WANT?

Eleni

MAMA LEANS away from the stove, where she's somehow managed to gather the ingredients for what she's calling "Italian Souvlaki" and meets my gaze.

"We have to buy those tickets soon, zouzouni."

I look down at the cucumber I'm grating for tzatziki. Three days have passed since I made my decision, and I still haven't told her. I don't know how. I know Mama should go, but I've never been away from her. She still wakes up in the middle of the night, shaking and muttering Baba's name. How can I look her in the eye and tell her that justice will only come to our family if she leaves alone? That I've let myself get roped into the same life that killed Baba?

"I have to go to the bathroom," I say.

She nods. "Just leave the cucumber by the sink. I'll squeeze it if you're not back in time."

I scurry out of the room without meeting her eye. Maybe, if I can actually get my thoughts in order, I can tell Mama tonight. She's in a better mood than she has been, and I caught her humming her wedding song without crying earlier.

"...so I think we should widen the radius," Tony says.

I freeze. The ornately carved door to what I've come to realize is Dante's office stands slightly ajar, something I've never seen in my days here.

"Do we have the bodies for that?" Dante asks. "I'd rather not waste time going back over places we thought we cleared."

My breath catches. I don't know what they're talking about, but I can tell it's mafia business. Which includes me now.

Tony murmurs something too low for me to hear, and then Dante appears in the crack of the door wearing another all-black suit. I stare up at him, half expecting the same dangerous heat to his voice I heard in his bedroom. Listening in like this has to be against the rules.

Instead, Dante opens the door wider. "Do you need something?"

I step back. "No, I don't want to interrupt—"

"Don't be ridiculous." He holds the door for me, motioning for me to come inside.

But I hesitate, my hand on the doorknob as I watch Dante cross the room.

He sits in a beautiful leather chair behind a wide, wooden desk with the same intricate carvings as the door. "We were just wrapping up. Tony, make the call, let me know when it's done."

Tony glances at me, and I think I see some emotion flicker in his eyes before he nods to his don and leaves. I have no choice but to step in and shut the door behind me.

Like so many of the other rooms in Dante's house, the luxury is overwhelming up close. What looks like a small office holds not only the beautiful desk and chair, but a few bookshelves stuffed with everything from modern thrillers to crisp nonfiction to faded novels that look like they'd fare better in a museum. Along one wall is a fireplace made of the white marble that covers the kitchen, which Gianna whispered to me the other day was called Carrara, like that was a name I should recognize. A low, dark fainting couch lounges in front of the unlit fireplace, and an armchair that looks like a smaller version of Dante's own sits in front of his desk. After a moment of deliberation, I take the armchair.

"So"—he steeples his fingers—"What can I do for you?"

"I need to buy Mama a ticket to Greece," I blurt.

"No, you don't." He taps a few keys and turns one of the monitors on his desk to face me. "I've got it handled. She leaves on my jet in three days with an armed escort. Parikia, right?"

I blink. "What?"

"You said she'd be safer in Greece." He leans closer, and I catch a whiff of his woodsy cologne.

My mind whirls instantly back to the shooting range, when that smell nearly overwhelmed me. His hand was so warm on my stomach, even through my shirt, and I want to know what those hands would feel like on my skin. But he keeps backing away. That could've just been the best way to teach a beginner like me to shoot. He might not have meant anything.

"Thank you," I say. "Please, let me pay you back."

He waves a hand dismissively. "You're a Saint now. I take care of my people."

But he doesn't look at me when he says it. Instead, his attention is already back on the other monitor, and I can't help but wonder what's on there.

"Mama's making Italian Souvlaki," I say. "If you want some."

He nods. "Can I do anything else for you?"

The question stings like a dismissal. I stand to leave, and he looks up at me. His dark eyes burn with a fire that could turn me to ashes. His gaze saunters down to my lips and back. Surely, he meant something. Surely, I should say something. I open my mouth.

And the words catch on my tongue. I'm not this kind of girl. He's a boss, and he already probably thinks me forward. I shut my mouth again.

Dante leans back. "A thought for a thought?"

"What?" I ask, embarrassingly breathless. I need to get control of myself.

"I'll tell you what I'm thinking if you tell me what you just chose not to say." He stands and strolls around his desk to lean on the front.

I nod, shove down years of trying to keep men's eyes off of me, and speak. "I was going to ask about the shooting range. About…the way you touched me."

His smile is warm and dangerous. "See, I was thinking how much I regret not taking you up on your offer at the auction."

My breath catches, and he seems to watch the movement in my chest.

"What are you thinking now?" he asks.

"That I shouldn't be thinking about your hands on my waist," I whisper. "That I shouldn't be dreaming about that kiss at the auction."

"Because I'm a boss?" He prowls a step forward.

I dodge around the chair and step back. "Yes."

"And bosses are dangerous." It's not a question, but the smirk on his lips makes me certain he's teasing.

"You're dangerous." I take another step back. "And you're not just any boss, you're my boss."

His lips tick up in a delighted smile. "There you go again, wanting me to own you."

I swallow. I didn't mean that. I think. My next step knocks the backs of my knees against the fainting couch, and Dante catches me the moment before I fall with an arm around my waist.

"Can I kiss you?" he murmurs.

My own warnings echo in my ears, but I just stare up at him. This close, his face isn't perfect anymore. I can see the bump in his nose where it was broken, a thin scar running from his upper lip to his ear. They only make him more human.

"You can do whatever you want," I reply. "You bought me."

He shakes his head indulgently. "I want to hear you say yes, El."

My blood turns to fire in my veins, and my knees go weak. I'm in the arms of a man who could destroy me without a thought, and he wants my permission to kiss me when I've been throwing myself at him for a week.

"Yes."

He brushes his lips over mine, feather-light, and I push myself up into him. Something ignites. He devours my mouth like I'm the last meal he'll ever eat. I gasp as he sinks his teeth into my lower lip, and I realize what I thought was fire before was only smoke, a promise of the raging inferno Dante could ignite in me. He lifts me and lays me down on the fainting couch, then kneels between my splayed knees. My skirt rucks up to nearly my thighs, and I can't bring myself to care.

"I said a thought for a thought." Dante stares down at me with a wicked hunger in his eyes. "You gave me two, and I don't like being in people's debts."

My breath races as he trails his gaze down my body to my exposed legs.

"I've been thinking I can't go another day without knowing what you taste like."

MORE

Eleni

MY MOUTH FALLS OPEN. The boss of the Staten Island Saints is licking his lips and telling me he wants me.

"I—yes," I say. "Please."

He smiles wolfishly and dives in to kiss me again. Distantly, I'm glad the fireplace isn't lit. Dante generates so much heat, ignites such a burn in me, that I think I'd disappear if the room were any warmer.

Still, somehow, I'm surprised when he runs his hand up under my shirt. He was warm at the shooting range. Here, his touch is a flame against my skin. I arch up into him as he grazes my ribs and sets off another cascade of heat.

"Responsive." He smiles as he kisses along my chin, down the line of my neck. "I like that."

His praise makes my heart hammer. I want him to smile with his lips on mine. When he gestures me up and grabs the bottom of my shirt, I don't hesitate. No one has ever seen me like this before, but it feels right to be Dante.

He pulls my shirt off over my head and starts to push me back down, but I reach for the clasp of my bra. His smell, his touch, his gaze, they're intoxicating. I want to give him all of me and more.

Dante doesn't stop me, just watches with wide, appreciative eyes as the white cotton falls away from my chest. He doesn't give me enough time to get self-conscious, either. His hands are on me before I've even laid back down on the couch. I gasp at the sensation. Despite the hunger in his gaze, in his mouth, he touches me delicately. He cups my breasts in each palm, though my flesh overflows his grasp, and kneads.

Another, softer gasp falls from my mouth as I grow used to the sensation of being touched. He studies me as he trails one finger up over my nipple, almost too light to feel. I bite my lip and let myself fall into his eyes. He nods and strokes it a little harder. I press up into him.

When Dante flicks my nipple, hard, the soft bite of pain mixed with pleasure shoots down my spine, and I make a noise I've never heard myself make before. I clap a hand over my mouth.

He grabs my wrist and pulls it away. "I've sound-proofed this room. I want you to moan for me. I need to know what you like." He presses a kiss to my palm and releases my hand.

"Will you?" I ask. "Make sounds, so I know what you like?"

He chuckles. "Ambitious. Why don't you wait and see?"

I start to pout, but he flicks my other nipple, and another moan pours out of my mouth.

"Better." He smiles and presses his mouth to my chest.

Between his teasing smile and the praise on his lips, my body hums before I even feel the wet press of his tongue. He suctions his mouth over one nipple and flicks the other absently with his thumb. The world starts to melt away, and I become nothing but heat and want. I wind my fingers into Dante's dark hair and yank his face closer, wanting more. He makes a low sound in his throat that vibrates through my whole body. The warmth between my legs burns hotter and brighter, threatening to burn me alive.

He releases my nipple and meets my gaze. "Are you wet, El?"

I flush. I took all the sex ed classes in high school. I know, at least in concept, what he's asking. But I never experimented. I don't know how to know. I only know about the wildfire inside me and my certainty that only he can quench it.

Dante seems to read at least some of this in my face. "I want you to put your hand in your panties for me." He leans up on his elbows so my arm fits between us.

He holds my gaze as I slide my free hand down my half-bare body to the waistband of my skirt, then under and into my panties. What I find there almost doesn't make sense for a moment. How, when I am nothing but fire, am I producing so much wetness? Because I'm soaked, all the way through my panties and probably onto my skirt. Maybe onto Dante's nice couch, so he can never forget I was here.

His eyes burn. "Well?"

One spot between my legs burns brighter, and I push my fingers against the hardened nub of flesh there. There is a loud, wet sound, and I see stars.

Dante grins. "Perfect."

He slides down my body, pushes my skirt up to my waist, and grabs the sides of my panties. I'm already nodding before he can look up at me for permission, my fingers still pressed against that nub, pulsating with desire. Cool air brushes over the wetness as he yanks my panties down and tosses them aside.

Dante groans. "I see you've already found your clit. Good."

He kisses up the inside of my thigh, sending off more cascades of want, and I grab his hair again so I don't drift away entirely. When he reaches the apex of my thighs, he moves my hand aside.

"Let me see your pretty pussy," he murmurs.

I sparkle with his praise. He'll take care of me. And then I'll lose my virginity, right here on this couch.

The first press of his mouth pulls a scream from my lips. I drag him closer by the hair as he circles my clit with his tongue, using the same firm, teasing strokes he used on my breasts. When he picks up speed, I wrap my legs around his head. The fire in my belly becomes blinding, racing toward an apex. An orgasm. As he sucks on my tender flesh, one thought takes over my mind: I need him inside me.

I tug on his hair until he finally pulls back. The lower half of his face glimmers with my wetness, and his gaze keeps drifting enviously back between my legs.

"I'm going to—" I shake my head. "I want you."

He strokes the outline of my…pussy indulgently. "You have me."

"I want you," I repeat, staring at his pants.

Realization dawns in his eyes, and a wolfish smile takes over his lips. "You want my cock."

I nod so furiously I can feel my breasts bounce, and he watches the movement until I stop.

"I'm not going to waste my first time inside you on this couch," he says. "No, when I fuck you, El, I'm going to have you completely undone and at my mercy."

His voice shivers down my spine. I want to be good for him.

But not that good. "I want more."

"I knew you were a hungry little thing." He kisses my clit. "But I promise the wait will be worth it."

He dives back in before I can respond. This time, when I go to clamp my legs around his head, he forces them back down, pins me open for his enjoyment. My moans echo off the walls of his office and return to me, desperate and needy, as he moves his tongue ever faster. I want—

The peak of the inferno hits me hard and fast. I scream Dante's name and yank his hair as overwhelming pleasure wracks my body in wave after wave. Every time I start to come down, his mouth is there, drawing it out a little longer.

Finally, I collapse, breathless and boneless.

He kisses the inside of my thigh and releases my legs. "You taste delicious, by the way."

21

NEXT FLIGHT TO PARIKIA

Eleni

TWO DAYS after my night in Dante's office, I sit on the king bed Mama and I have been sharing with my knees curled up to my chest. I haven't seen more than a glimpse of him since then. He helped me dress, made me promise to go to the bathroom, gave me one last searing kiss, and then…nothing.

"I feel ridiculous." Mama turns from the closet that was slowly stocked with clothes in her size and preferred style over the last week with a sweater in her hands. "I should just take everything, yes? Even if I'll never wear it back home?"

"You should take whatever you want, Mama." I smooth a pair of pants in her open suitcase. "You never know if you might travel someday."

"It is free." She looks at the bright blue sweater. "What are you packing, zouzouni?"

I have gotten good at not flinching when she asks me questions like this. I really did mean to tell her that night. But when I walked away from Dante with my knees still weak and told her about the ticket, she threw her arms around me with tears in her eyes and started talking about our fresh start. How we'd never replace Baba and Christos, but we could figure out how to be happy in the world they left behind. And then I meant to tell her the next day, but she showed me a list of things she couldn't wait for me to see in Parikia. And that's how I ended up here, the day her flight leaves, without saying a word.

I don't know if I've spent more time worrying about her or Dante in the last two days. Every glimpse I have gotten of him, he's with Tony, or Tony's brother, or another dour-faced, crisp-suited man. Something is going down. I just don't know why no one will tell me what.

"You shouldn't let my choices dictate yours," I say.

She shakes her head. "You're no help."

Despite how lightly she means it, the comment stings. I will help our family by staying. I just know it.

Finally, Mama decides to pack half of the winter clothes Dante provided, just in case, and we walk down the stairs to the front door, where a car should be waiting to take Mama to the airport.

"Are you excited?" she asks. "I always thought going back home would feel like losing, but with you by my side, I can't wait to see my little hometown through new eyes."

My stomach churns, and I hum noncommittally. I'll tell her at the airport, when it's too late to change anything. It's selfish, the worst thing I've ever done to Mama, but anything else will kill me. I swing open the door to see a black SUV and Tony's brother leaning against the hood.

"Hey." He jogs up the couple front steps to grab Mama's suitcase. "I don't think we've officially met yet. I'm Sebastian, but my friends call me Seb."

"Eleni, but you already know that," I reply.

He half-bows to Mama. "So that makes this your…sister?"

Despite his obvious dramatics, she giggles. "I suppose it's nice to know some Made men have manners."

"I still believe in chivalry, miss." He hefts her suitcase and grins. "You're in safe hands."

Even I smile at his antics. Seb seems much easier to get along with than his older brother.

"Oh, zouzouni, you left your suitcase upstairs," Mama says.

My heart skips a beat. My skin turns to ice. I forgot about the suitcases.

"What suitcase?" Seb asks. "She's not going anywhere."

The world feels like it's moving in slow motion as Mama looks from him to me. Whatever she sees in my face makes her eyes fill with tears. Then, her brow furrows as she gets angrier than I've ever seen her.

"Tell me this young man is wrong," she says quietly.

I can barely hear her over my heartbeat in my ears. "I can't, Mama."

Seb mouths, "Sorry," over her shoulder.

"I raised a smart girl," she says. "Your baba raised a smart girl. Where is she, huh? What have you done with her?"

"I'm right here." I put my hands up like I can ward off her words. "I thought it through, and someone needs to make sure the Lombardis pay—"

"Pay?" she screeches. "You are starting to sound like these monsters. Where is my zouzouni, my little bug? Because I know she knows that no amount of payment, no amount of revenge, will return Baba and Christos to us."

I take a step back. "We don't know that Christos is dead."

"I raised a smart boy, too." She towers over me like she hasn't since I was little, since I surpassed her by an inch in high school. "After two years, either my Christos is dead, or I don't know him anymore. Give up this *vlakódis* plan and get in the car!"

My eyes sting with tears. "I can't, Mama. I can't let them win."

"Eleni Calimeris, you get in that car!" She crosses her arms. "Or I don't."

My chest squeezes. "You can't stay. You're going to get hurt—"

"And you won't?" She grabs my arms, and for a moment, I think she's going to shake me, but she just crushes me to her chest. "I can't lose you too."

"You won't," I whisper. "I'll make sure of it. And Dante will, too." His name tastes like ash in my mouth. "He takes care of his people."

She pulls back to meet my gaze. "You joined them."

I can't lie to her now. I nod.

She drags me back into the hug and strokes my hair. "I love your baba, but he still had a few old prejudices rattling around in that brain of his. He was determined to make Christos into his successor, to have him lead the family. But you've always been the spitting image of him. Stubborn. Ridiculous." She kissed my hair. "Determined to break my heart."

I shake my head. "This is new. I was the daughter you and Baba wanted before this."

She laughs wetly. "You are always the daughter we wanted."

Mama squeezes me one last time and lets me go. When she looks at me, I can't shake the feeling she's memorizing my face, like she's already decided this will be the last time she'll see me.

"I love you," I say.

"I know that," she replies. "And I love you too. I just…."

She lets her sentence trail away, then turns and joins Sebastian in the car he fled to when Mama started yelling. They pull out of the driveway, and my chest aches. I am not the last of the Calimeris family, but in an hour, I'll be the last in America. It's an even lonelier thought than I expected.

I'm still standing on the steps, staring at the driveway, when Gianna leans out of the open door behind me and says, "I think Dante might actually kill you if you let any more heat out."

I jump and turn. She's wearing the thin, striped shorts and matching oversized shirt I've come to recognize as her pajamas, despite the late afternoon sun already descending toward the horizon.

"Oh, shit," she says. "Was today…?"

I nod. My chest hurts like my ribcage is trying to claw my heart out. I don't cry.

"Oh, hon." She wraps me in a hug, and I let her because I don't know what else to do. "I know it's hard now, but it'll get easier."

"When?" I mumble.

She rubs my back. "Hard to say. But I know a way to make it go faster."

I look at her.

"Come out with me tonight!" she grins.

I agree because I don't know what else to do. Maybe a distraction will be good.

2 2

DRUNK

Dante

I shoulder open my front door long after everyone in the house other than Gianna will be asleep. My own silent halls greet me. I kick the door shut, nudge off my shoes, and head upstairs to shower before I get blood on anything important.

It's been two long goddamn days, but Thano's people are finally starting to close in on a potential location for Luca. Tony pulled them in more after I told him to make his own call. Yet another good decision that night. I stride into the master bathroom attached to my bedroom, strip, and put my suit directly in the second laundry basket I keep in there for anything that needs serious stain removal. Then, I switch on the massive rain shower I splurged on a few years ago.

Everything's been moving too fast for me to check in with Eleni, but after how vocal she was in my office, I get the sense she'd let me know if I'd done anything wrong or pissed her off. Once we have a location on Luca, I'll bring her in as an operative, but we've finally cracked enough skulls that I can carve fifteen minutes out of my day tomorrow to talk to her. Or whatever else she wants.

I step into the steaming spray and run my hands through my hair. The black tile on the floor and walls doesn't show the blood draining off my body, which makes it that much easier to let my mind drift to Eleni's fingers where mine are. I'm used to being in charge in the bedroom—and in most things—but I can't quite bring myself to mind the way she pulled me around. The little sparkles of pain were appealing in a way that made me understand submissives for the first time in my life.

Just the thought of her makes my cock start to harden, and I groan. I have been spending far too much time jerking off while daydreaming about a woman who seems to want me just as much as I want her. I don't want to push her into anything she's not ready for, but I'd be happy to spend another night between her spectacular legs.

When all the blood is gone, I step out of the shower, turn it off, and pull on a robe. Her mother left, according to Seb, so maybe she won't mind a wakeup call. I grin as I march down the hall to the spare bedroom she chose, leaving the door to my room open behind me.

I knock on her door. "El? Can I come in?"

No answer. She might be a heavy sleeper. I can picture her sprawled across the bed, drooling slightly on the pillow. I knock a little louder.

Still nothing. The hair on the back of my neck starts to rise. I push open the door, calling her name softly, and my stomach drops to my toes.

Empty bed. No Eleni.

I race through the rest of the house, checking room after room, to no avail. She's not here. Gianna isn't either, but that's normal. Suddenly, my normally empty house feels cavernous. I sprint back to my room and grab my phone to dial Tony.

"Do you have Eleni?" I bark as soon as he picks up.

"Nope," he replies. "Why, is something up?"

"Later." I hang up. Seb was supposed to circle back to the house after making sure Maria got on the plane safely. I punch in his number.

The phone rings, and rings, and eventually goes to voicemail.

I straighten as certainty sends iron down my spine. Luca struck first. He has Eleni. I dress quickly and calmly, hiding guns and knives in all the inner pockets I had added to my suit, then call Tony and a couple other capos to meet me at the house. I'm halfway through dialing Thano to put the search for Luca on hyperdrive when my phone rings.

Sebastian.

I answer immediately.

"Hey, boss," he says a little sheepishly.

I blink. He doesn't sound pained. There's no rasp to his voice like he's been gagged or dehydrated. I hear thumping bass in the background.

"Do you know where Eleni is?" I ask.

"Yeah." He swallows audibly. "Big drama with her mom, Gianna asked if she wanted to go out, and Eleni said yes."

My stomach finally starts to rise from the pits of hell it descended to. "Piacere?"

"Where else?" I can hear Seb's grin. "But, uh…you should know Eleni's kind of a lightweight."

<hr>

"LIGHTWEIGHT" is the understatement of the century. She's shitfaced.

I nurse a much-needed scotch at one of the high tables next to the dance floor and look at Eleni. She's in the middle of the crowd, moving like a thing possessed and wearing what is probably the most modest of Gianna's dresses. The sparkling pink fabric drapes to her knees, due to the difference in their heights, but it pulls taut over her breasts and ass. Sometimes, Eleni dances with the same sinuous grace she displayed on the couch in my office two nights ago. Other times, she loses the beat entirely and collapses onto Gianna. Somehow, both of these coax my forgotten erection back to life. I haven't really seen Eleni laugh yet, not with the full-throated abandon I can sense from here. I've barely seen her smile when she's not mocking me. Now, she looks carefree, like any other twenty-three-year-old on my dance floor.

My slow sips of scotch fail to calm my imagination. I indulge in a fantasy of joining her out there, of her weight against my chest as she grinds into me, of teasing her to the edge of orgasm in the middle of the crowd and then whisking her into a back room to see how loud I can make her scream with all her inhibitions lowered.

A douchebag with over-gelled hair appears out of the crowd and rolls his hips against Eleni. She turns to him a little muzzily and seems to try to push him away, but he holds on, rucking up the skirt of her dress.

My vision goes red, and I am striding through the crowd of dancers before I realize what I'm doing. A few of my men positioned around the room drift forward. They think I've spotted a threat. Good. I want this man, and every man like him, scared.

When I reach them, Gianna looks at me, goes pale, and opens her mouth to say something. I ignore her and turn right to the douchebag.

"Get your hands off of her," I say very calmly for the fury burning in my veins.

"Or what?" He laughs.

"Dante?" Eleni sways, and from this distance, I can see how blurry her gaze is. Only the barest remains of a dark pink lipstick clings to her mouth, the rest surely left on too many glasses.

"I wouldn't ask me questions like that if I were you." I give my voice a dangerous edge.

He rolls his eyes and yanks Eleni against him. "Fuck off, buzzkill."

I slam my fist into his throat. The douchebag stumbles back, coughing. The crowd begins muttering. Gianna grabs my arm and says something I can't hear as my world narrows to Eleni, now unsupported and confused.

Without a second thought, I lift Eleni, toss her over my shoulder so she can't see the rage on my face, and stride into the back hall.

23

DANGER

Eleni

I BLINK AWAKE, not remembering falling asleep or the slick leather under my cheek. Music still pounds into my hazy skull, but much softer now. The last thing I'm certain of is dancing at Piacere, and then…Dante?

"I know you're awake," he says from somewhere in the room.

I sit up, and the room blurs like I'm in a cartoon until I'm upright. Mostly upright. My eyes catch on a wall clock that says it's one in the morning. Then, I see Dante behind a crisp, modernist, black-glass desk. I blink a few times. Nope, he doesn't look happy.

"So?" I lever myself to my feet. Gianna convinced me to wear one of her dresses and a pair of her heels, so standing is even more of a challenge than it otherwise might be. She also convinced me not all alcohol tastes like the crap Dante drinks, and boy was she right about that.

"So," he repeats. "So, Luca Lombardi is still out there. You're in danger, Eleni. Do you get that?"

"Yes," I say with total confidence. I recognize enough of those words to be completely confident that once the room stops spinning, I will absolutely get that. "Can we go dance now?"

He scrubs his hands over his face. "No! We can go home, where you're fucking safe."

"Safe this, safe that." I lean on the front of his desk and watch his gaze fall to the front of my very tight dress. "I want to have fun for once."

"You can have fun when Luca Lombardi is dead." He grits his teeth and forces his gaze away from me.

The haziness in my head gives way to the clarity of anger. "And who are you to make that decision for me? I haven't even seen you in two days."

"Your boss." He smirks at me. "Remember?"

"Uh-uh." I shake my head, despite the way that makes the room shift like a boat. "Nope. If that's the deal, I want out. Because I've lost my whole family to this life"—I circle around his desk and poke him in the chest—"my whole family, now that Mama's gone, and if I can't have them back, then I deserve a few frickin' drinks."

He grabs my wrist. "Since when do you say words like 'frickin?'"

"Since—" Never. But I couldn't let him know that. "Forever! Because I'm living my own frickin' life now, not just trying to make people happy."

He exhales sharply through his nose. "Do you want me to treat you like a prisoner, El?"

His grip on my wrist tightens, and the whole argument tumbles out of my brain. He's so close, and his eyes are burning, and it turns out anger and desire look pretty much the same through however many pretty pink drinks I've had. I lick my lips and lean in.

Dante swallows. "I could force you to do whatever I said. I could use you however I saw fit. And if you insist on breaking my rules and putting yourself in danger like this, I just might have to." His voice descends to something between a growl and a purr.

I sit on his lap, bracketing his legs with mine. "Promise?"

He groans. "You're—"

"Trouble." I pull my wrist out of his grasp and put his hands on my breasts.

He runs his thumbs over the fabric, and my nipples harden instantly. None of my bras "worked" with the dress, according to Gianna, so she loaned me a stretchy, lacy bralette. Between that and the thin dress, I can almost feel his hands on my skin already. I rock my hips against his lap and feel his hardening erection.

"Please," I whisper. "I'm done waiting. F-fuck me."

His gaze goes dark and liquid, but he says, "You're drunk."

"I haven't been this clear-headed in…maybe ever." I stabilize myself on the arm of his chair so I don't disprove my point by toppling over. It doesn't really matter if I'm a little drunk. Or mad at him. I wanted him when I was sober and happy. I want him now.

Before he can say anything, I kiss him. Like a spark on tinder, he's instantly alive underneath me. He presses his tongue into my mouth, exploring every crevice and tangling with my own. I moan and rock against his lap, against the length of him between us. I didn't get to feel him last time, and his size strikes fear and desire into my heart in equal measures. Dante groans into my mouth, and I swallow up every note. Someday, I'll make him yell. Maybe tonight.

Roughly, he pulls the top of the dress down, and my breasts bounce free. The bralette Gianna loaned me is stretchy, but the lacy triangles still leave most of my skin exposed. Dante stares for a long moment.

"We're getting more of these," he mutters.

I like the sound of "we."

He twists and flicks one of my nipples, sparks of pleasure-pain clouding my vision more than any alcohol, and drops kisses along the line of my neck. When I tilt my head back and moan, he sucks a dark bruise into the skin there. Another sweet sting. My thighs are parted over Dante's legs, but in the few places they touch, I can feel them starting to slide. I'm more than wet enough.

I grab Dante's free hand, braced on the arm of his chair, and guide it between my legs. "I'm ready."

He pulls my underwear aside and slides a finger through my wetness with a smile. "So you are."

His fingers find that hot, bright point of want, my clit, and circle it. I collapse my weight against him. Sensation pours through me, near overwhelming, and supporting myself is too much. He chuckles and doesn't stop. When the fire in my gut starts to build to that breaking point again, from nothing but his fingers, I struggle for the words to tell him what I want. When they don't come fast enough, I twist my head and bite his earlobe.

He laughs. "Hungry?"

I nod. "Please."

His fingers slow, and I roll my hips to hold onto the pleasure.

"You're a virgin." He shakes his head. "I don't—"

"I do," I say. "I don't need rose petals or candles or whatever. I just want you."

I struggle to sit up and look into his dark eyes, but even as my orgasm drains away, my balance is still off. I end up with my forehead pressed against his, breathing in the same air he's breathing out.

"I want you to be my first," I whisper.

Taut silence hangs between us, and I begin to hope. He's not saying no.

"El—"

A high-pitched trill interrupts him. He glances around for a moment, then grabs his cellphone off the desk.

"Cattaneo," he says, his voice suddenly brusque like it wasn't a moment ago. "Mm-hmm. Yeah. Okay, I'll be there soon."

2 4

PATCHING UP

Eleni

WHEN DANTE TURNS back to me, the heat in his gaze is dead. "I have to handle this."

"Yeah." I pull my bralette back over my bare chest, and the dress over that. "Of course."

He watches me like he wants to help but doesn't know how. "I'll have Seb take you home."

I climb off his lap and try not to feel like the stupidest woman alive. After a few moments, Seb opens a door I didn't notice and leans in.

"I'm sorry—"

Dante just nods at me. Seb shoots me an apologetic smile, and I walk out with him.

"So, have I pretty much ruined my chances of you ever liking me?" he asks as we walk up the stairs to the main club.

"Between this and Mama?" I smile wryly. "We'll see."

Pretending to be normal with Seb is the only thing keeping my emotions from overflowing. I don't even know where they're going to go anymore. I can just feel them, corked and bubbling in my chest.

He chuckles and holds open the door to outside. I step into the cool night air and rub my arms until he pulls up the car he drove Gianna and I here in . Feeling restless, I climb into the front seat rather than the back.

"Radio's all yours," he says. "Especially if you tell Dante this was Gianna's idea tomorrow. I'm trying to make capo someday."

The mention of Dante sets my blood boiling, so I turn on the radio and crank up the volume on the first station that comes in clearly. I don't want to hear anything else Seb has to say.

When he drops me off in front of the house, it takes the three steps up to the door for my emotions to crystallize into potent anger. Dante keeps pretending to be this super cool mob boss like I can't see the way he looks at me! Like I couldn't feel his cock when I climbed in his lap! I know he wants me. Sometimes, like when he asked for permission to kiss me, I start to think he might like me. But he's too scared to do anything about it.

I storm up the stairs and start to head to my room, but a new idea pops into my brain. He thinks he can just keep getting rid of me. Well, I'll show him I'm not going anywhere. I stride down the hall to his bedroom, throw open the door, and flip on every light I can find. As I expected, he has a private bathroom, and I need a shower before bed. I turn on the faucet and strip quickly. Gianna's pink dress that I probably stretched out. The flimsy bralette I hope I never see again. My still-soaked panties. The stupid, ribbon-laced heels come off last mostly because I struggle with the ties, and then I launch myself into the shower.

The still ice-cold spray shocks most of the remaining alcohol out of my system in a second. Showering in here is silly. But I'm not exactly going to get out now. I scrub myself as quickly as I can, trying not to let the smell of Dante's products coax me into visions of him joining me in here and finally having sex with me, then climb out.

I might be sober now, but I'm still pissed. I leave my clothes on his floor and all the lights on, but I resist the instinct to fall into his bed naked. He doesn't deserve that.

***

I ROLL over in bed for the hundredth time, and a sliver of light peeks in through my eyelids. I pry one open and the light is sunrise. A quick check of my phone confirms that five a.m. has come and gone. No sign of Dante yet.

At least my head has stopped spinning every time I move. Gianna made me drink water between every cocktail, so a small headache pounds between my eyes, but nothing serious. And the tan sheets on the bed are soft against my skin.

I can only come up with two reasons for him to still be out, and my brain keeps fixating on the "he hates me now" one. Something could've gone wrong with his business, but I know how I must've looked. Half-dressed even before I let him make a mess of me, grinding on his lap and begging for him. I looked like a slut. The thought sends me burrowing deeper into the blankets, like I can just make the whole night go away.

The front door opens. I sit up. That has to be Dante. Do I go out to see him? Does he want anything to do with me? The front door closes slowly, but not like he's trying to be quiet. Like he's holding onto it. His footsteps on the stairs stumble out of time, and my heart leaps into my throat. I don't care what he thinks of me. I have to know if he's okay. I pull the sheet off the bed, wrap myself in it, and race out of the room.

There, at the top of the stairs, stands Dante. His lip is split and swollen. His knuckles drip blood onto the stairs. I can't see his jacket anywhere, and his shirt is pulled part of the way open, exposing a triangle of fine, dark chest hair. My mouth falls open, and I rush to him.

"What happened?" I demand.

"You know that douche I punched?" He stares down at me, some unknowable emotion in his eyes.

I nod.

"Turns out the douche had friends." Dante wipes the blood off his lip. "Biker friends. So I had to convince them Piacere wasn't their kind of club."

My heart hammers, and I grab his hand to look at his split knuckles, remembering at the last second that I have to hold onto the sheet. "You shouldn't have done that. I know a little bit of first aid. Let me clean you up."

"You giving me orders now?" he asks with a crooked smile.

I shake my head and tug him down the hall toward the general bathroom. Too late, I realize my mistake. His gaze catches on his open bedroom door, then drops to me. There's a feral hunger in his eyes, wild and wanting.

"You're certainly not taking them." Faster than I can follow, he snatches the sheet from my grasp.

I can do nothing but stand before him, naked and outlined in the golden light of his bedroom. He looks me up and down slowly, absorbing every detail. For a cold, terrifying moment, I think he's going to dismiss me again.

"My bed," he says. "Now."

25

───────

GREEN

Eleni

WARM DESIRE COILS between my legs as Dante stares at me, his eyes burning and proof of my disobedience behind me. Part of me wants to run to his bed, to do whatever he asks. The rest of me wants to know how far I can push him.

I cross my arms under my boobs, pushing them higher. "Make me."

His gaze turns impossibly darker. "Green if you're good. Yellow if you need a moment. Red if you need me to stop."

I blink. "What?"

He prowls closer. "I'm going to take you apart, El, and I want to hear you scream. We need these words so I know when you're serious. Repeat them."

"Green if I'm good, yellow if I need a moment, red if I want to stop," I say, not really understanding but liking the hunger in his voice.

"Good." He smiles.

He snatches me and throws me over his shoulder. I don't even have time to yelp before he's racing down the hallway to his bedroom. I cling to his rumpled shirt and feel the wind cool my already wet pussy. I've released something in Dante with these words that I can't put back. And I don't want to. He throws me down onto his bed roughly, making the mattress bounce. His gaze drags over my body.

"Don't you dare cover yourself," Dante says. "I bought you. I can look at you whenever I goddamn please."

I bite my lip and squirm as desires burns.

"But I'm going to have to teach you." He strips out of his shirt and sits on the bed next to me. "Over my lap."

I sit in his lap like I did in the basement of the club and lean in for a kiss.

He covers my mouth. "Have you earned that?"

I swallow and search his gaze for real anger. Nothing but desire. This is part of his game, part of the cuffs on his bedposts and the words he taught me. Part of owning me. I shake my head.

He grabs my chin. "You might be teachable after all." Dante pushes my face nearly into his plush bedspread and my hips into the air. "You've earned a punishment. Ten with my hand. Let's see how long it takes that ass of yours to pink."

I squirm, but his grip is iron. I couldn't escape if I wanted to.

His first hit lands sharp and bright, right on my...ass. I yelp, and he massages the sore flesh until I moan.

"Good." His praise is honey sweet. "Still green?"

"Bright green." I wriggle my ass. "Emerald."

"Another for squirming." He spanks me again, this time on the other cheek.

I jolt forward and barely bite my tongue against a comment about how I can keep going. I want, no, need him to fuck me. The next hits land back and forth, and my skin warms. The desire in my gut only grows. I'm his, and if I break his rules, he'll take me up here and remind me of them.

At eleven, he cups my pussy. "Are you sure you learned your lesson? It seems you may need more."

I nod furiously.

"Show me, then." Dante releases his grasp on my waist. "Get on the bed."

I scramble off his lap, my ass burning almost as hot as the want between my legs, and lay across the middle of his bed. He doesn't move for a long moment, and I grow nervous. When minutes tick by, I cover my breasts and sit up.

"Dante?"

He whips around with a feral smile. "What did I tell you about covering up?"

I have to swallow down my own smile at his ploy. He wants to push me to the edge. He wants me to be in trouble. I wrap my arm tighter around my breasts, jam a hand between my legs and almost gasp at the friction, then look meaningfully at his pants.

"You're covered up."

"Because I make the rules." He rips my hand off my breasts and drags me up the bed to lock it in one of the cuffs. The leather is warm and soft around my wrist, almost comforting.

"And you follow them." He tears away the hand between my legs.

At the burst of pleasure from movement, I moan his name.

"Oh, you want something?" He smirks. "Good girls get what they want."

He locks up my other wrist and strips out of his pants unceremoniously. I stare. I knew Dante was beautiful, but naked, he looks like a god. His olive skin clings to taut, powerful muscles. Ink black hair lays in fine curls over his chest, then thins into a narrow line that connects to the bush around his lengthening cock. My mouth waters and falls slightly open.

"Next time." He taps my bottom lip.

I suck his finger into my mouth and cup my tongue around it. He tastes sort of salty and musky, and I realize with a jolt that's my own wetness. Then I wonder what Dante tastes like. Next time.

He slides fingers through my wet folds again. "We didn't finish earlier, did we?"

I shake my head around his finger. He pushes another one past my lips.

"Then this should be easy." He attaches his mouth to my neck and begins toying with my clit at top speed.

The suddenness of his movements catches me by surprise, and I hook my leg around his waist as my orgasm races forward. Just as suddenly, he goes still, and I whine.

"Good girls get to come." He smiles wolfishly. "I'll fuck you when you've earned it."

I gasp around his fingers, and he starts to fit another one inside, then pauses and pulls back.

"Green?"

"Green!" I grind into him and stretch my tongue out for his fingers.

Dante smirks and begins undoing me, just like he promised. He brings me to the edge of orgasm a second time, a third, a fourth. He thrusts his fingers so deeply into my mouth I start to gag and he promises me I can take it, have to take it, if I ever want his cock in my mouth, and oh god, I do. When he says my mouth is ready, he takes those same fingers and fucks them into my pussy one at a time, stretching me around lubrication I provided. When he stops after the fifth edge, three fingers inside me, I collapse to the mattress.

"Please," I whimper. "Please, Dante, I just want your cock."

"Pretty little thing." He smiles down at me. "How could I deny someone who begs so well? I think you finally understand that"—he bends down to whisper the final few words into the shell of my ear—"I own you."

His voice shivers down my spine, feeling nothing more than right.

"I'm yours," I gasp. "Please."

With his fingers still inside me, he reaches over and withdraws a condom from his nightstand, then slips it on. I keen as he finally starts to pull out, aching from the loss of him.

"Just a middle step." He lines his cock up at my entrance. "Green?"

"Green," I almost weep.

He starts pushing in. Immediately, I realize what I thought was just torture was actually careful preparation. My walls stretch, burn just a little, but they don't snap like everybody always said they would. Instead, Dante slides home like he's always belonged inside me. I was right to pick him for my first.

I look up at him, ready to beg more, but a change has come over his face. He's no longer the hard, domineering man he's been since he gave me those words. Instead, he looks at me in awe, like I'm something beautiful he can't quite believe he gets to touch.

"Dante?" I ask.

He snaps his hips forward, a tiny thrust, and I gasp.

"Call me Sir in here." He grabs his hips. "And say thank you."

"Thank you, sir," I murmur as he rocks into another tiny thrust. I'm already so close. "More, sir, please."

He grabs one of my breasts and begins slamming his hips against mine. My long-awaited orgasm flares to desperate life. He flicks, twists, tortures my nipples, slaps my breasts like he did my ass, and everything drives that moment of perfect pleasure ever closer. I thank him for every touch, words garbling around moans in my mouth.

"You're so good," he hisses.

And I'm coming. An explosion of pleasure so bright I can barely feel my body arch, can barely hear his grunt as he goes still with me, the pent-up power of five delayed orgasms whirling through me like a lightning storm.

When I finally regain myself, he has already rolled off and to the side. I tug on the handcuffs, rattling the chains.

"Are you going to let me out, or can we do that again?"

2 6

———

THE MORNING AFTER

Dante

THE NEXT MORNING, I wake in my rumpled sheets to a warm presence beside me. Eleni. For a small woman, she really does stretch out. Her hair, shining red-brown in the morning light, covers a whole pillow, so she's stolen a corner of mine for her head. She's on her stomach, so I can't see her truly spectacular breasts, but my memories of them make me consider getting into sculpture because breasts like that deserve immortalization in marble. What I can see is the curve of her ass, just disappearing under the blankets and still a little pink from her first punishment, and the possessive hand she has on my chest.

Possessive might be too strong of a word. She's taking up more than half the bed. I could just be in her way. But I like to think it's possessive. She was incredible last night, a natural submissive who danced between bratting and obedience in a way that made me never want to go to sleep, but when I slid into her for the first time, something changed. She wasn't just the sexy as fuck woman I've been trying to resist for weeks. She was…something I've never seen before.

115

My chest aches even as my cock starts to respond to memories of last night.

Last night? What the fuck am I saying? I came home at basically dawn and fucked her into my mattress until the sun had already come up. I have to get my ass out of bed.

I ease myself out from under her hand, and though she grumbles and rolls over, she doesn't seem to wake. Her adjustment reveals a small drool spot on the pillow that makes me smile.

No! I'm not smiling! I'm kicking my ass into high-fucking-gear because Thano was closing in last night, and I'm not gonna miss out on a chance to drop Luca just because I had great sex. I rush through getting dressed in one of my many all-black suits and sprint out the door to grab the phone I know I left in my car last night.

"Oh, Sleeping fucking Beauty joins the party," Tony says as I reach the top of the stairs. He lounges in the sitting room with a view of the open stairs, flipping through something on his phone.

"Long night." I join him downstairs. "Did I miss much?"

He hands me a hot espresso. "You can say that again. Thano found the bastard."

I shoot the espresso and wince at the burn. "Fuck."

"Car's ready outside." He hands me a to-go cup of coffee and my favorite pistol. "I was gonna wake you, but you seemed to already have a roommate."

I glance at him. His smile is teasing, but not pointed. He might've opened the door to see me in bed with someone, but he didn't recognize Eleni. Thank god.

"Wake me next time," I say because that's what I would've said if it were anyone else. "I don't have anything you haven't seen."

"I saw everything you have in that one club in Atlantic City." Tony rolls his eyes as we stride out of the house.

I laugh, and the conversation drops. I'll tell him soon. Right now, though, I need everyone focused on splattering Luca Lombardi's brains against the nearest wall.

I hop in the driver's seat of the car Tony already started, the armored SUV with the bulletproof glass, and tear out of the neighborhood as quickly as I can without waking anyone after Tony joins me. Out here, it's easy to tell I didn't sleep as late as I feared. The wan winter sun is still high in the sky, and a quick glance at the dashboard clock tells me it's barely afternoon. My bruises from last night ache, and I'm exhausted, but the jet fuel coffee Tony brought starts to put a little pep in my step.

"I'm ready to end this." I pull onto the thankfully empty Verrazano mid-workday. Just us, a minivan, and a little shit-colored sedan behind us.

"Seconded." Tony fixes his already perfect hair in the mirror.

"You're pretty enough." I nudge my caporegime as we turn off the bridge and GPS leads me through a few tight turns.

After the first, the shit-colored sedan is still behind us. The hair on the back of my neck prickles. I take the second and check my mirror. Still there.

"I think we've got something stuck to our shoe," I murmur.

Tony and I draw our guns in unison as I take the third turn into a tight alley of a road that leads nowhere but the place we're going, after one last T-intersection. The shit sedan turns after us. I nod at Tony, but the sound of a car accelerating rips through the air.

"What the—"

The sedan leaps forward and smashes into the back of the SUV. I snap forward, my neck springing back and forth like I'm a fucking bobblehead, but the armor plating holds. Tony and I twist to start shooting through the back window.

Fucking mistake. The shit sedan keeps flooring it, shoving the SUV forward. I squeeze off a shot, shattering the glass, and stomp on the brake to no avail. They put something else under the hood of that piece of crap. The gears whine, but we keep racing toward the wall of the T-intersection. Tony fires shot after shot. I fight with my seatbelt to reach the parking brake.

As soon as the nose of the SUV enters the T-intersection, two more cars gun at us from either direction. Metal screeches, crumples. My seatbelt snaps against my chest. Tony hollers, but my ears are ringing too loudly for me to know what he says. Arms work. Head feels like a bowling ball that just rolled a strike, but all my thoughts are in order. Legs—

"*Cazzo!*" My left leg is completely pinned and hurts like a mother-fucker. My right's in a rough spot, but I think it'd hold my weight. "Tone?"

A round cracks into the bulletproof glass, but not through. We have a second.

"Still breathing." I hear the rattle of him reloading. "Better than you, I think."

Another round. The glass on my side turns into a spiderweb of cracks. I glance at Tony and find he's right. He could get out, if he had the space.

"Ambush." I tuck my gun out of view of the window bitterly.

He growls something under his breath, and the glass shatters. Someone reaches in through Tony's window and opens his door, but I can't pay attention to that. A broad man with a gold tooth grabs my collar and begins yanking me out.

"Jackass." I pull my gun up and fire a round through his throat.

A smaller man behind him charges forward, and I drop him with a bullet in the head. I'm not going to waste my ammunition on the bulky body armor they're obviously wearing under their suits. Then, I turn to check on Tony.

Three men, as big as the first I dropped, have him by the arms and are dragging him back to the shit sedan.

"Motherfucker." I try to rip my left leg out of its prison but only succeed in nearly making myself scream from the pain. Something's seriously wrong.

Fuck it, I don't need legs for this. I twist in my seat, ignoring the next burst of searing pain, and wait for the men holding Tony to enter the oval of the back windshield.

One, two, three. Like shooting fish in a barrel, they fall. Tony salutes me through the back window and hops in the shit sedan to try to get me out.

It takes some maneuvering, but eventually, all the cars are far enough away that Tony can crowbar open the driver's side. I tumble out, and he catches me. As expected, my left leg can't hold any weight.

"Jesus." He catches me. "Maybe you should've stayed in bed."

I snort. "Check their fucking pockets, chuckles."

He deposits me in the relatively un destroyed backseat of the SUV, and I look at the cars. All completely average, shit-colored sedans. But the SUV crumpled like a tin can, so someone fucked with their innards. If these cars were what they looked like, they wouldn't be able to touch us. And, I realize, none of them have license plates.

Tony jogs back over with a couple cellphones in his hands. "You want the bad news or the worse news?"

I heave a sigh. "Bad."

Tony grimaces. "Thano Coppola set up the ambush."

My stomach drops. "Well, what the fuck is worse than that?"

He holds up a flower-patterned case. "One of these guys took his wife's phone to work."

I drop back on the SUV seats with a groan.

27

BOILING POINT

Eleni

I SCROLL down a page on my online textbook and glance at the clock on the dining room wall. Nearly one. When I woke up in bed alone, I was a little frustrated. Last night was nothing short of magical for me, but I've seen movies, so I know what sneaking out before the other person wakes up means. When I searched the whole house for Dante and didn't find him—or any note—I was worried. I know he's a boss, and that means he's always going to work weird hours, but this much of a rush in the middle of a weekday seems strange.

But now, as I sit at his massive, luxurious dining room table trying and failing to do homework for night classes I haven't been to in what feels like years, I'm downright scared. There's no sign of Dante except an espresso cup with a thin film remaining at the bottom. I talked to a couple of the staff, and one of them said Tony rushed Dante out as soon as he woke up, so he's obviously not kidnapped or anything, but it's been an hour, and I feel like I'm losing my mind.

What if something happened to him? What if I committed myself to this life, to revenge, and all I end up with to show for losing myself is one great night of memories and the knowledge that Luca Lombardi is never going to see punishment. I slump back in my chair with a groan. Life was so much easier when I was just the good daughter my parents wanted, not trying to find my own definition of good.

The door slams open, and I leap to my feet. Stumbling into the front hall is Dante, leaning heavily on Tony's shoulders. Both of them look like they've been in a fight. My heart races, and my breath catches, but I need to try to seem like I haven't spent the last hour worrying about him.

"If you're gonna make a habit of busting your knuckles on people's faces, I'll start keeping a first aid kit by the door," I say.

Dante doesn't even look at me. My chest stings. As he and Tony drag themselves past, more men pour through the door, men I don't recognize. All of them wear suits and have the same crisp bearing I'm used to from the men in the Staten Island Saints, but this is more than I've ever seen. And like a rushing river, they're all headed for Dante's office. My stomach flips. Something huge happened.

"What's going on?" I ask the nearest man.

Like Dante, he doesn't even seem to hear me. I ask again and again, and no one turns. I hear the name "Coppola" in their conversation, but that doesn't mean anything to me. I just end up standing off to the side, watching them race by like another piece of Dante's beautiful furniture.

Eventually, the stream starts to dry up. I glance at the still-open door and see Seb silhouetted there. He, unlike everyone else, makes eye contact with me as he steps inside.

"Can you see me?" I ask with a half-smile that hopefully doesn't look as emotionally all over the place as I feel.

He nods but pulls me aside with a serious look. "You need to pack your things and come with me."

"What?" I pull my arm out of Seb's grasp. "Come with you where? I'm not going anywhere. I'm a Saint, just like the rest of you."

He shakes his head and looks away. "Safe house upstate. Boss's orders. I really can't disobey, okay?"

"No." I walk down the hallway toward Dante's office, following the end of the trail of men. "You heard wrong. Dante wants me in there."

"Come on, Eleni, don't make me the bad guy," Seb pleads.

We round the corner to Dante's ornate door, closed again. But as we stop, it opens, and my heart leaps. Of course, Dante didn't sleep with me and immediately cut me out.

"Peaches," the guy in the doorway says. "Get your ass inside."

Seb ducks his head. "Be back soon. Seriously, pack up."

And he walks through the door. The man has to open it a bit wider to allow Seb access, and I catch Dante's eye across the crowd.

I don't know what to expect. Warmth? The awe he looked at me with when he took my virginity last night? Anger? Even just recognition?

Whatever it is, I don't get it. I'm not really looking at Dante. I'm looking at the boss of the Staten Island Saints, and whatever Dante said, that man doesn't know me.

The door closes between us, and I storm upstairs.

"House in upstate," I mutter. "Can't disobey."

Last night, I was just playing around. I can show him what real disobedience looks like. I'll pack the bag he wants so badly and leave on my own. I'll—I'll—I'll go back to the apartment and just wait for Luca to show up. I'll take one of the guns and kill him myself. Then, Dante'll have to realize what an asset I am. He'll have to stop dropping me as soon as something else comes up.

I slam into my room and stare at the bed some of the cleaning staff made so neatly. Even the sheet I wore last night is back in place, as though it never happened. My chest squeezes, and I force that hurt into the same boiling anger. I yank the suitcase that appeared at the same time as Mama's out of my closet and begin throwing clothes inside.

When I'm fighting with the zipper to close it, someone knocks on my door frame, and I whip around. Dante, leaning heavily on the wood and looking like he got hit by a truck.

"What do you want?" I demand.

"Seb said you were upset," he says. "I came to check."

"Yes, I'm upset!" I release the suitcase, and the top springs open, undoing all my progress. "What happened to being part of your organization?"

Dante purses his lips. "The less you know about this, the better."

"Right, because I'm so uninvolved." I whirl back to the suitcase and begin fighting with it again. "Which is why it's totally safe for me to go out in the city—oh wait!"

Dante sighs. "You're being unreasonable. I'm trying to keep you safe."

"I don't want to be safe!" The zipper catches on a blouse, and I yank it with a small tearing sound. "I want to protect my family. I want to have a life! Did you know I have a final next week? I need to be here to take it."

"We can figure that out." Dante purses his lips, and I realize abruptly that he's holding something back from me.

"Just say it." I yank the suitcase the rest of the way zipped and sit on it. "Who the hell else am I going to tell, right? I don't have a life anymore."

He clenches his jaw. "El—"

"No." I meet his gaze. "I thought I wasn't supposed to actually be your prisoner."

He stares back at me, becoming the boss of the Staten Island Saints again. "Things have changed."

2 8

UPSTATE

Eleni

I GLANCE at Dante out of the corner of my eye. After he dropped the bomb about the situation changing, I expected him to explain or something, but he only took my half-packed bag and loaded it into his car. He drove me away from his house in Staten Island a few minutes later, and we haven't exchanged a word since then.

"Fuck, Philadelphia?" Dante says. "I was really hoping…no, no we can handle it."

That's not to say Dante hasn't been talking. He's spent the whole drive with his phone cradled between his shoulder and his ear, taking increasingly intense phone calls. This is the first mention of Philadelphia, and I have no idea what to make of that. The Lombardis only operate in New York, or so I thought. It's hard to think of anything beyond how absolutely furious I still am.

He spins the wheel and pulls into a long, horseshoe-shaped drive. A house emerges out of the trees. Like in Staten Island, it's not huge, but it's beautiful. This one has a deep, rich wooden exterior, like it's trying to blend in with the nature around it.

I hate it immediately.

Dante stops the car and climbs out, still talking on the phone. I press my feet into the carpet and wonder if I can just refuse to get out. My mind flashes back to last night—can it only be last night?—and the hazy memory of him carrying me through his club. Maybe, if I could just activate that side of him again, he'd realize how much of a mistake he was making.

He opens the door and stares down at me. "Yeah, fifteen to the north side. It'd be stupid to send any less."

It's like he's looking through me. The light in his eyes has been replaced by shadows, and his brow pinches dramatically together. My heart crashes to my toes, and I climb out without a word. I owe Baba and Christos getting back to New York City and seeing this through, but it seems there might be nothing for me in the Saints.

He leads me inside, handing me the key once he's unlocked the door, and I trail after him into a spacious living room styled like a log cabin. Finally, he hangs up his phone.

"I'm taking the car back to the city," he says. "The key in your hand opens every door in the house but the garage, and the nearest town is several hours walk away."

"So I really am a prisoner." My voice sounds small to my own ears.

"No," he says, "you're a person in danger who I can't trust to make the smart decision and stay fucking put."

I sit on a leather couch. "Great. That's a lot better."

Dante sighs. "Lock the door behind me. Seb will be here soon. Talk to him if you need anything."

He starts to leave, and my heart rattles against my ribcage like it's trying to go with him.

"Dante," I call.

He pauses in the doorway.

"Just…tell me what's going on. What changed?" I try to meet his gaze, but he avoids me like he's spent years practicing.

After a long moment of silence, he turns and towers over me. "What changed is that I am working on a way to get you out of this, and I can't do that with you in my house."

The words land between us, heavy and intractable. I turn them over in my mind. His brow is pinched again in a way I know means danger, and maybe not just for me. Dante—all of the Saints— might be in trouble. Part of me wants to forgive, to see Baba's straight-backed certainty as he marched into the living room for the last time in Dante's refusal to tell me anything. But I'm starting to understand why Mama told me I was always more like Baba. I don't care if Dante thinks he's right, or brave, or noble. I deserve the right to decide my own life.

I stand so he can't tower over me any longer. "Who says I want out?"

Dante's face goes stony. "I do."

"That's not your call." I step around the chair, frustration building. "It's mine. I got myself into this. I told you I wanted, needed, revenge on the Lombardis for what they'd done to my family. And you said yes! So why, all of the sudden, am I some fragile treasure you hide away upstate?"

"I never should've said yes," he replies.

I take a step back like I've been hit. There is no mercy in his dark eyes.

"You've made a lot of reckless choices El—eni." He shakes his head. "Not reckless, stupid. You never should've put yourself between your family and the Lombardis in the first place. Then, neither of us would be in this mess."

"This mess?" My eyebrows shoot up. The night we spent together crowds the air between us. I'm not going to bring it up first. If he regrets touching me, he can find the guts to tell me himself.

He runs a hand through his hair and glances around the living room like he's looking for something to save him. I just wait.

Finally, he says, "Word has spread about my new pet. The Lombardis aren't the only outfit sniffing around you now."

I bristle at terminology I know would've turned me liquid only yesterday. "So tell them I'm not a pet. Tell them I'm a member of your organization, just like anyone else!"

He pierces me with his gaze. "Did you even think about what

might've happened if I hadn't bought you at the auction? Or if you'd ended up at someone else's auction?"

I barely smother a flinch at the intensity in his words. "I figured I'd have to lose my virginity to a sweaty older guy."

"You have no idea." He takes a step closer to me, pinning me against the arm of the chair. "You could've been kidnapped, assaulted, any of a million things. I run a voluntary virginity auction, and I'm the only one in the goddamn city."

"So, I wouldn't have ended up at someone else's auction!"

"No, El, I run the only voluntary one." He stares down at me, trying to bore knowledge into my skull. "There are dozens of skin auctions and underground networks whose bread and butter is kidnapping and selling women with fathers, brothers,"—he swallows —"lovers in the mafia to the highest bidder. Hundreds of women, taking the fall for something their family did."

My anger banks. No, I hadn't considered that. I didn't even know that happened. I shivered at the thought of Leo, or worse, Luca Lombardi owning me for life. But Dante didn't say this happens to everyone. Just women connected to mafiosos.

"So?" I asked. "I'm not important to anyone in the mafia."

Something flashes behind the cold mask of his gaze, and he takes a step back. My heart skips a beat. Did last night actually mean something to him?

"Just…stay here," he says as he turns away again.

I stare at his retreating back. After all that, he's leaving?

When he reaches the door, he turns around again. "I'll have you back in the city for your final."

He shuts the door behind him with a click that echoes through the whole empty house.

29

___

RUMOR MILL

Dante

A FEW DAYS after dropping Eleni off upstate, I sit in the cheap, plastic chair of the Sing Sing Correctional private visitation room and eye the guard standing in the corner. He's not our usual guy, but Hank promised this guy would be just as good.

"I'm Dante," I say to fill the silence before my prisoner arrives.

He grunts. "You bring the shit?"

Certainly not the conversationalist Hank is. I pull the plastic-wrapped Cubans out of my inside jacket pocket and slide them across the table. The new guy picks them up, sniffs them, and they disappear in a crease in his uniform, in the way every prison guard I've ever met seems to have mastered. I've never been inside myself, and I'm not looking forward to that day, if it ever comes. I knock surreptitiously on the engineered-wood table and hope that's enough to scare away the bad luck.

The door buzzes, then opens to admit Uncle John, with his wrists and ankles chained together as always, and another guard. The new guy nods to the guard escorting Uncle John and takes over. The

129

escort looks me up and down. I smile my most innocent smile and spread my arms to show I even submitted to the indignity of changing into sweatpants for the visit because I accidentally got rid of my only pair of suit pants with no metal fixtures. The escort leaves, and Uncle John looks at the new guy.

"No Hank?" he asks me, still looking at the guard.

"Daughter's birthday," I reply. "But I figured this visit couldn't wait."

The new guy grunts and unchains Uncle John's wrists.

Uncle John sits, rubbing his wrists, and sighs. "No, it couldn't. You have anything for me?"

I pull out a pack of imported Italian cigarettes, and Uncle John snatches them up.

"Christ, this is the good stuff. I'm not even going to trade these." He smiles at me. "All right, Dino, I'm not gonna waste your time."

I don't look at the new guard to see what he thinks of the old family nickname.

"I've heard the rumors," he continues. "I knew you were scrapping with the Lombardis, but what the hell are you doing getting the Coppolas on your ass? You slumming it in Jersey?"

I crack my knuckles. Uncle John got caught a couple months before Frank Lombardi took out my dad, so he still thinks of me as the heir apparent, not the king.

"Thano set me up," I say. "He fed us crap information, and when Tony and I went to check it out, a handful of Coppola goons jumped us."

Uncle John blows out a long breath through his teeth. "Why were you relying on Coppola information in the first fucking place?"

"I needed more eyes." I shake my head. "But that's not the point. The point is, Thano claims he didn't know about the set-up. Fucker claims he didn't even know about the information Tony got, and I'm not stupid enough to buy that."

Uncle John nods. Gianna mostly got her mom's looks, but I can see a little of her in Uncle John. The greasy, salt-and-pepper curls could've turned into the mane Gianna obsesses over, and he's got the same way of holding his head when he doesn't quite believe someone. The same way he's holding his head right goddamn now.

"What?" I ask.

"Nothing." He shakes his head and looks away.

"You think I'm stupid?" The plastic chair creaks underneath me as I shift. "I know he could be telling the truth. He could have a mole in his operations, planted by the Lombardis or someone else. He could be playing me against Luca so he can swoop up the city when it's done. I'm still looking over my shoulder."

"Shit, Dino, I said it was nothing." He shakes a cigarette out of the pack and holds it up to the guard for a light.

The man grumbles but flicks a lighter until the end catches. Uncle John takes a deep drag.

"I guess I'm just wondering why you needed the Lombardis fast enough to bring in outside help," he says through his exhale.

Because the first day I walked into the Greek Corner, Eleni took my breath away.

No, it was more than that. She's beautiful, and smart, and aggravating enough to keep me up at night thinking about what the fuck she's going to do next, but she's also…normal.

My whole life, I've been the prince of the Staten Island Saints. That is, until I became the king. I can't look twice at a girl without every outfit worth knowing about between Boston and Trenton catching wind of it. That first day in the restaurant, I didn't feel any of that. I was just Dante, and she was just Eleni. No title around my neck, no blood on my hands.

I told her at the house that she was making stupid choices, but I was the real moron. I'd let my heart lead me since that moment. Even at the auction, I sprang into action so goddamn fast because I wanted to protect that little bubble of normalcy, to keep her out of this life. And then what did I do? I held the door right open and invited her in. If anything happens to her now, it'll be on my head, and I'll burn the world to ash before I let anyone get away with that. Maybe I'll burn the world to ash anyway. Coming home to an empty house these past few days has been so much worse than I expected.

But I can't tell Uncle John that.

"I was sniffing around for anything that would give me the in to revenge Dad," I say, "and an innocent got caught in the middle. She's in danger until I tie this up, and I'd rather not waste manpower on bouncing her from safe house to safe house because I'm dragging my feet."

Uncle John tilts his head again, and I know he can tell I'm playing fast and loose with the truth. I just hope he hits on the safe house stuff I'm saying because this new guard isn't vetted like Hank and not anything about Eleni.

"An innocent, huh?" he says. "I heard a little about this innocent. Heard her name was Calimeris."

I swallow a grimace. It's not good that her name made it all the way to Sing Sing. "So?"

Uncle John shakes his head. "You've always had a soft heart, Dino. This is about Christos, isn't it?"

My stomach flips. "No."

"Uh-huh." Uncle John smiles teasingly. "Don't worry, I won't tell that the boss of the Staten Island Saints is a softie."

I stand. "You and I both know that the number one thing Dad taught me was to always pay my debts. If this were about Christos— which it isn't—I'd be paying my dues, not going soft."

"You done already?" Uncle John raises his eyebrows. "I thought we were gonna shoot the shit."

"I have places I need to be." I nod at the guard, who re-cuffs Uncle John. "Call me with any further rumors you hear."

"I'm not in here much longer, Dino." He stands.

He has a month left on his sentence. The guard buzzes the door, and I stride out. I have nothing to say to Uncle John about any member of the Calimeris family.

30

IN THE WIND

Eleni

After a few days of wheedling, I've finally convinced Seb to walk with me around the property. His car is locked up in the garage, and if Dante's right about how far the nearest towns are, there's no point in me running. So, I'm stomping through what I can only call woods in shorts I've never worn before and an oversized T-shirt, and somehow still sweating enough that I'm sure I must smell and Seb's just not mentioning it. Spring came early to upstate New York, and a hot spring at that.

I crunch a stick under a pair of steel-toed combat boots I found in the depths of the suitcase I packed. Yet another thing that just appeared in my closet. I've never worn anything like them in my life, but they're incredible for stomping.

"I'm surprised," Seb says.

I glance at him and have to suppress a snicker. He's trying to do the same hike in a full suit, and he's red as a tomato. Maybe that'll keep him from aimlessly flirting with me for a little while. I don't really mind it, but I've never been more bored, so I'll take anything new.

"Surprised how?" I ask.

"I figured a city girl like you would be sunning yourself by the hot tub, not clomping through the woods."

I shake my head. "Just because I don't know anything about plants doesn't mean they scare me. I'm less worried about what I'm going to step on out here than I was in my back alley at home."

"Fair enough." He glances at me out of the corner of his eyes. "I'm also surprised you actually pried yourself out of your books long enough for this."

I grimace. My final is right around the corner, and I should be plastered to the wi-fi disabled laptop Seb brought up with him. But I still can't quite believe Dante's promise that he'll get me back in time. He's abandoned me up here for days now, and I don't even have a phone to check in with him. Seb is my only connection to the outside world.

"Ah, I know that look." He grins. "Slacker?"

I shake my head furiously. "Never. Do you know how much these classes cost?"

"Not really." Seb wipes sweat off his forehead. "The most book-cracking I ever did was when I fucked a girl into a library shelf hard enough that a few books fell off."

I shake my head. I can't decide if Seb's a ladies' man or a wannabe, but he has more of those stories than I thought someone my age could.

"A lot," I say. "Enough that I can only take two a semester."

Seb whistles. "That...sounds like a light load?"

I smack him gently, falling into patterns from before Christos disappeared, then recoil when my knuckles impact metal.

He winces and pulls a gun out of his jacket. "Sorry. Seemed better to be safe."

It doesn't seem like there's anyone in this forest with us other than birds. "I won't complain if you let me shoot it."

Seb screws up his face. "I don't know...."

"Baby." I shake my head and return to hiking.

"Shit, fine." He hurries to catch up. "But only when we reach the edge of the property. I don't want to find out Dante has some kind of antique tree that I let you kill."

Always worked on Christos.

"But in exchange, I wanna hear more of your school shit," he says.

I glance at him. He gives me puppy-dog eyes, and for the first time in days, I almost smile. Maybe he's just curious because he didn't pay any attention.

"I'm going for a computer science degree," I say. "But with only two classes a semester, it's gonna take me forever to finish." I kick a stone out of my way and watch it tumble through the trees. "Two classes if I actually make it to my finals."

"This might sound stupid, but...why do you care so much?" Seb asks.

I swallow. I can't tell him about the fights Christos and Baba had when he dropped out of school. Christos swore he'd spoken to a real recruiter for a professional football team, and as long as he went now, he'd be guaranteed a spot. Baba pulled out curses in Greek I didn't even know yet and said Christos was throwing away the real opportunity of a lifetime, an education. Mama and I sat on her bed together, both pretending not to listen.

"I'd be the first person in my family with a degree," I say finally. "And my parents really wanted that for...the family."

Seb nods quietly. "Yeah, I get doing what the family wants."

Before I can ask what he means by that, he stops dead. "Edge of the property."

I stare at him in confusion until he offers me the gun. Right. I'm no longer the good daughter who waits while her family fights. I'm the stubborn bitch who's going to get our revenge. I take the gun from Seb.

"Hit that tree." He points at one maybe ten or fifteen feet away.

I take aim, trying not to feel the ghost of Dante's hand on my waist, and shoot. Bark flies.

"Nice!" He points a bit farther away. "That one next."

I shake my head and hold the gun out. "I want to see what a real Staten Island Saint can do."

The words burn on my tongue, but Seb grins. Just like I thought. He never really believed I was in. I don't even know if Dante told anyone.

Still, we trade shots back and forth, each trying to outdo the other, until he points at an oak in the far distance.

I check the cylinder. "Two bullets left. You first this time."

He lines up his shot with a smile and just clips the very edge.

"He shoots, he scores!" Seb fakes a cheering crowd as he celebrates.

I shake my head and take the gun. "Have you ever fired that thing in a real fight? Like, killed someone?"

Seb holsters his gun with a sigh. "Nah. I've fired, but I haven't killed anyone yet. I can't become a capo until I do."

I aim. Inhale. Know you want to take that life. I fire, and bark explodes off the trunk.

Seb stares, stunned. I approximate his celebration.

"When I kill someone, will I become a capo?" I tease.

"Absolutely not. Girls still aren't allowed, and the amount of time it's gonna take you to fight that will let me get my kill in first." He snatches the gun back, grinning.

"Hey!" I swing out, half for the pistol and half just to hit him.

He sticks his tongue out and takes off through the woods. I chase him through the trees, trading easy insults until we both have to slow down because we're laughing too hard. It's been a long time since I laughed.

We emerge out of the trees nearly in unison, and I shout, "I'm gonna make you regret that, Bellini!"

Seb freezes, staring at the porch, and I turn slowly. Dante stands there with his hands on the railing. And he doesn't look happy.

31

DANGEROUS

Eleni

"Go to the driveway, Sebastian," Dante says without even looking at me.

"Of course," he replies. "But my car—"

"Tony is waiting there to drive you to your nonna's. You're both expected in the city for a family dinner." Slowly, like the action pains him, Dante drags his gaze over to me.

My smile dies on my lips.

"Cool." Seb starts jogging away, leaving me alone with the fire-breathing dragon, then stops. "Uh, is Eleni gonna be safe? Am I coming back?"

Dante grits his teeth. "I'll make sure she's safe. Go."

Seb shoots me a quick, apologetic shrug and leaves. I cross my arms and stare up at Dante.

"Safe how?" I ask.

"I'll be staying here tonight." He turns away without another word.

I gape at the space he left for a moment, then race after him, through the back door. He has to know that he can't avoid me for a whole night. The house is bigger than anywhere I lived before Dante, but it's not that big. Maybe he's ready to give me answers. I find him in the kitchen, unpacking three full grocery bags. The food startles me. If he's only staying for a night, why did he bring so much? Seb was talking about stocking up soon, but Dante struggles to fit another bottle of milk next to the one already in the fridge. I open my mouth to ask.

"What were you and Sebastian doing?" he asks icily.

"Going for a walk." I grab the two different boxes of cereal and put them in the cabinet next to the one Seb and I had been sharing.

"How far?" he asks.

"Just the property line." I glance at Dante to see him turning quickly away from me with a scowl on his face. "We weren't running away together. Seb's devoted to becoming a capo."

Dante's scowl deepens. "I didn't think you were running away together. That would be ridiculous. I've only been gone three days."

I give up on the groceries and cross my arms. "What would you being gone have to do with me attempting to escape exile?"

"Not you," Dante says testily. "You and—"

I stare at him for a long moment. "Are you jealous?"

"No." He keeps putting groceries away with robotic precision, like I'm not even in the room, he won't even look at me. "There's nothing to be jealous of. You said it yourself. You're not important to anyone in the mafia."

I grit my teeth against the sting. I'm starting to learn the rhythms of fighting with Dante. If he's lashing out like that, I've hit on something. My heart flutters. If he's jealous that means—

That means nothing. He could just want to sleep with me again, maybe exclusively, and not anything else. But I still want to know.

"Seb took me shooting." I watch Dante closely.

His whole body stiffens, though he forces himself to keep moving. "Is that what he was going to…regret?"

"Part of it." I take a step closer. "Why do you care?"

"I like to know what the people in my organization are up to," he bites out.

"Uh-huh." I lean against the counter. "And what does that have to do with pathologically denying yourself any emotions?"

He whips his head up to look at me. "What are you talking about?"

"You're jealous," I whisper. "Admit it."

"Why do you insist on throwing yourself at every dangerous thing in a five-mile radius?" he mutters as he turns away.

I bristle. "I wasn't throwing myself at Seb."

"I'm sure he'll tell a different story." Dante shakes his head.

I pluck at the front of my shirt, pulling it away from my body, as old hurts run through my head. I should've known Dante would think I was easy too.

"I get it," I spit. "You like me as long as I'm the innocent little virgin, swayed by your bad-boy charm. If there's another bad boy, forget about it."

"No, I—" Dante grimaces.

"Newsflash, I'm a real person." I start walking away from him. "I'm not just a toy you can pick up and put down whenever you feel like. You have to decide what you want from me, Dante, because I know what I want. I broke up my family to get this revenge. I'm all in."

"El—"

I turn back and glare at him. "What do you want?"

He runs a hand through his hair. "I want to know why revenge is so important to you that you'd throw your life away."

My breath catches. All of the coldness is gone from his eyes. He's burning up like the night we spent in bed together.

"Today was very nearly the first time I've seen you smile." He takes a step closer to me. "You've smiled drunk. And on the verge of orgasm. Nothing else. And I—"

I bite my lip. My heart pounds out of time.

"I am trying to protect you because I hate that you're in this situation." He takes another step closer, mere feet away. "But I hate even more that I'm glad you're here. That I didn't want you in Greece with your mom, I wanted you next to me, in life-threatening danger, because I'm selfish, El."

He looks at me with those burning eyes again, and all of my higher brain functions shut down. I don't think about the days he's been away, about my anger or my isolation. I don't even think about how smelly I must be after that hike. My legs start moving even before I've given them the order, and I launch myself at Dante. My mouth crashes down onto his.

Dante puts his hands on my hips, and for one terrible moment, I'm certain he'll push me away. Then, he slides one arm fully around my waist, crushing me close to him, and flicks my mouth open with his tongue. The world stops turning around us. He kisses me so intently that I bend backward before I even think to break away.

Finally, he pulls back for air. He's panting, his eyes already half-lidded, and I can feel him hardening against my leg. I want to see more, to have the next time he promised. But my heart skips a beat, and I have to be sure.

"Last time we did this," I murmur, "you left."

"I don't want to leave." He lifts me up and kisses me again.

I wrap my legs around Dante's trim waist, and his suit slides between us. He carries me, step by step, through the kitchen. I have no idea where he's going, and I don't care. He's not leaving. That's all I need.

The backs of my thighs meet cold stone as he pushes me up onto the counter. I don't release my legs. I can't give him the space to step back, can't lose any point of contact with him. I even wind my fingers into his dark hair to pull him closer as my lungs start to ache. Breath comes second on my list, right after inhaling Dante.

He cares. I wasn't just making everything up, misreading his signals, pursuing a man who'd throw me away like garbage. He cares, and I've finally gotten him to admit it.

Dante fights my grip to escape my kiss, but gently, like he doesn't really want to go. My lungs are screaming, the feeling tingling down between my legs, but I draw the moment out a few seconds longer before letting go. My chest heaves as I suck in fresh air.

"Breathe." He nods. "Maybe another day. For now, I want to know how I can make this up to you."

I open and close my mouth a few times. I just want him. He knows all the sex terminology, the code words and methodologies. But he just lets me flounder.

"I want what you promised me," I say finally.

3 2

BREATHLESS

Eleni

I WATCH Dante dart into the connected living room to grab a pillow from the couch.

"For your knees." He sets it on the floor.

I swallow. Dante watches the movement with hungry eyes. Slowly, I kneel on the pillow instead of the tile floor. His suit pants bulge in front of my face, and I lick my lips. Time for my first blowjob.

"What next?" I ask.

He smiles and unfastens his pants, then shoves them down with his underwear to pool on the floor. His cock springs free. I'm pretty sure it's bigger than last time. He wraps his hand around it and pumps a few times, until liquid beads on the tip.

"You can go slow," he says. "Trust me, it's just as good slow."

I lick the bead of liquid before I can overthink it. His flavor bursts over my tongue, salty and musky and Dante. I hum.

"Good." His voice sounds tight. "Now put your hand where mine is. You don't have to take it all."

I cup his length, firm but springy under my palm, and he groans. I don't need any more instructions. I lean forward and take his cock in my mouth.

He clenches a hand in my hair, sparks of sharp pain joining the want in my gut, and I circle my tongue around him. That makes him clench harder, moan again. I bob forward, taking another inch, and immediately, the feeling is all-consuming. He barely hits the middle of my tongue yet, but all I can taste, smell, and see is Dante. I look up to meet his gaze, and pure, animal hunger burns in his eyes. I bob a little farther and synchronize with my hand.

My name falls from Dante's lips like a prayer. I close my eyes and devote myself to making it happen again. Every time I go forward, I take a little more, always remembering his fingers in my mouth, opening me up.

I hit the beginning of my gag reflex, and tears fill my eyes. Dante starts to pull back, and panic leaps through my veins. I grab his ass and go farther, take more. The tears spill. My lungs start aching again as I pull in thin breaths through my nose. It's just like kissing him. Breath comes second.

"Green?" he whispers.

I nod. Next time I move forward, he moves with me, taking more of my mouth. I moan, and he groans in response. My lips meet my hand. Only a few inches left. I am burning up, so full of him there's almost nothing else, but I'm nothing if not determined. I release his cock and grab his ass with both hands. Farther. I gag just a little, calling more tears. I can do this.

When I bury my nose in his thatch of dark pubic hair, the pleasure that breaks through me is nearly orgasmic. Dante cares, and now he knows he can't tell me what to do. I can always take more. I look up into his eyes, just holding him inside me, and there's no way to describe the expression.

"I'm close," he murmurs.

I dig my nails into him and roll my tongue along the underside of his cock, panting. Breathless. A few moments later, he stiffens, and hot liquid pours into my mouth. I forget to swallow, cough, and he pulls back. Come spills over my lips. Before he can ask, I lick it up.

"Jesus fucking—" He shakes his head and yanks me to my feet, claiming my mouth.

I am alight, moving against him, tasting his tongue and his come in one breath.

"Do you like this shirt?" he asks against my lips.

I shake my head. Something clicks, and with a sound of ripping fabric, Dante slits my shirt up the middle. The two halves fall away, and he yanks my bra cup aside to torture one of my nipples. I moan his name. Warm air whisks against my bare skin, and I press myself close to him. I can feel his soaked cock against my leg, just below the hem of my shorts. He's not ready to go again yet, but I'm sure we can find a way to fill the time. I tear at the buttons on his shirt, wishing I had the knife to strip him.

He puts one of my hands on the breast he was torturing. "If I do your part, you have to do mine."

I twist and tug my aching nipple as he whips through the buttons and sheds his shirt and jacket. He pulls off my bra. His chest hair rasps over my bare skin. I moan and start to memorize the patterns that send waterfalls of want between my legs. I've never touched myself like this before. He pushes me back a step, and I obey, hoping he abandons his pants behind us.

Another step, and he unbuttons my shorts. They fall away as we walk to show my plain cotton panties. Then, Dante reclaims his position on my breast and shoves his other hand between my legs, over my underwear. I gasp up into him as I hit the back of the couch. It only takes a few circles before my first orgasm threatens.

"I'm close," I say, just like he did.

"Good." He shoves my underwear aside and slips two fingers into me.

I shriek his name as pleasure overtakes my senses. But unlike all the other times, he doesn't stop and let me relax. He just releases my clit and keeps thrusting his fingers into me.

I stare up at him, panting and helpless.

"You mentioned the shooting on purpose." He shakes his head. "That means you need a punishment."

I blink. "I thought you were apologizing."

He wipes a bit of his come off my lips. "I was."

Then, Dante spins me around and bends me over the couch, ramming three fingers into me. I yelp his name and grind my hips back into him, a second orgasm already on the horizon. My breath races as it takes me, and I shudder around him. Still, he doesn't let me up. My third peak rattles my bones. I pant against the couch cushions. A distant part of me wants to kiss him again, but as he wrings more pleasure out of my body, I realize he is still everything I can sense. There is nothing else.

After the fourth, he holds a silver packet in front of my bleary eyes. "Open it."

My hands shake, but I rip the foil open. He pulses his fingers inside me as he slides the condom on one-handed.

"Who do you belong to?" he asks.

"You," I gasp.

"You, who?" I can hear the smile in his voice.

"You, sir," I rock back onto him. "Please."

"Since you said please." He rips his fingers out of me and replaces them with his cock so quickly I barely feel his absence. "Play with your tits."

I moan and pluck at my nipples again, driving my oversensitive body even closer to the edge. He slams into me, knocking my hips against the back of the couch. I come again before he's even close, and when I lose my grasp on my nipples, he smacks my ass once, sharply, then bends over me to take them in his own hands.

My world has dissolved into the scratch of his chest against my back, the pounding pulse of his cock in my pussy, when he starts thrusting jerkily. He wraps a hand loosely around the front of my neck and pulls me up like that until we're both standing, then kisses me. My breath disappears.

Dante mouths my name against my lips as he comes, and that is enough to send me over the edge again. I collapse onto the couch when he pulls out, boneless and sated. He drapes a blanket over my mostly naked body and kisses my forehead.

He's not going anywhere.

3 3

CAT AND MOUSE

Dante

I STARE at El for a long moment, just watching her chest rise and fall under the blanket. As soon as she wakes up, I'm going to need to hop on aftercare. She's been remarkably resilient to the power dynamics so far, but I won't risk anything happening to her out of my laziness. I grab my phone and head upstairs, still naked, deciding to run a bath and then wake her.

She picked the biggest room. Rebellious. I know she doesn't care. Still, I head into the oversized bathroom and turn on the tub.

As the water pounds against the surface, my thoughts drift. Tony isn't taking Seb to their nonna's, though I'm sure he'd love it if he was. No, Tony got a lead on some guys connected to the ones who jumped us, and I decided—for some fucking reason—that he should take Seb, and I should come up here. I pour myself a glass of scotch from the liquor cart in the bedroom and shake my head. I should be in the city, prowling the streets for Luca. We keep just catching his scent, then losing it again. Like he's fucking taunting us.

My phone rings. I grab it off the counter and answer without checking who's calling.

"Hi, Dante," Tony says in the slow tone of voice I know means he has someone he needs to scare the shit out of in the room with him.

I shut off the tub and wander back downstairs with my drink. "You found the shitheads, then?"

"Roger." There's some shuffling on the other side of the phone, and someone yelps. "Yeah, I got 'em, and they're in a talking mood."

"Wonderful." I let my voice drop low and hungry as I step into the living room where Eleni sleeps. "What are they saying?"

"They're saying Thano didn't send them."

My stomach churns around the scotch. There's no goddamn way. They were Thano's people. He must've sent them.

"I can vouch for that." A new voice crackled over the phone line from a bit away but clearly in the same room, and it takes me a moment to place the voice as Thano himself.

"Yeah, you would vouch for that, wouldn't you?" I snap. "Makes your life real goddamn convenient."

Eleni stirs, frowning and pushing the blanket until her breasts are mostly exposed. My mouth goes dry, and I take a step away.

"Well, then how can I prove it to you?" Thano asks, his voice clearer now, like Tony handed him the phone.

I grimace and sip my drink. He's a slippery son of a bitch, and even with Tony there, I struggle to come up with sufficient proof.

"Look, I'm just as pissed as you are," he says. "Some Lombardi snake wiggled its way into my nest and poisoned my men against me. You dropped the first few, but now I'm left with the fuckers who let the snake in."

"Then prove your loyalty," I hiss.

For a breathless second, nothing happens. Then, three gunshots rattle over the line.

"It's done," Tony says.

In the background, I can just make out Thano telling another person in the room to clean this fucking mess up.

"He says he has something real on Luca," Tony mutters.

I sip my scotch. Everything real turns into smoke. Maybe I've been wasting my goddamn energy trying to chase Luca.

Maybe it's time for the mouse to become the fucking cat.

"I don't want it," I say.

Tony snorts. "Funny. You able to get back into the city for dinner?"

I ignore his question. "Look, what happened when we lost my dad?"

"Everyone was aimless. Took a while to get the Saints together under your thumb," Tony says slowly. "Which means if Luca doesn't show his face soon, he'll start losing people."

I raised my glass as if Tony could see me. "Exactly. Tell Thano to keep an eye but sit on it."

And my silence, especially if Luca left this opening on purpose, will drive him insane. I grin, and stress sloughs off me. He's the new kid on the block. He should have to chase me. Eleni stretches and bares herself to the waist. My mouth waters.

"Done," Tony says.

"And no, I won't be back for dinner." I set my glass down on the table. "Expect me back on Thursday."

He says a quick goodbye and hangs up without questions. He's stopped asking them about Eleni. But it's hard to care about that when she's right in front of me, pliant and nearly naked. I slide onto the wide couch next to her, my cock already hardening. She barely stirs. I take one of her breasts in my hand, marveling not for the first time how she hides these under the modest clothing she seems to prefer. They're like a wet dream in themselves, flesh spilling decadently between my fingers. And all mine. I circle her rosy nipple with a finger lazily, watch it start to harden. A quick glance at her slack face tells me she's still asleep, but her cheeks are starting to pink. Just like her ass did, that first night.

My cock aches, and I palm it to soothe a little of the pressure. There's so much I want to do with her, to her, and she seems to want it just as much. But for now, I just want to see the look on her face when she realizes I'm fucking her awake. Thursday is the day before her final, just enough time to get settled in, and that means we have three days in private up here. I intend to take my time with her.

I lower my face to her other nipple, savoring the feeling of being surrounded by her breasts, and flick my tongue across it. She gasps, and I glance up. Still sleeping. God, she's incredible. I tease her flesh slowly, gently, never sharp enough that the pain might wake her. She shifts in easy rhythm underneath me, murmuring shapeless syllables like she's talking to someone in a dream. Perhaps she's dreaming of me.

I smile and pull the blanket fully away from her body. She frowns, but I cover her in myself before she can get cold. With one hand still on her breasts, I kiss down her chest to the panties I never got around to removing. They're still soaked, a fact that pushes the aching in my cock into the stratosphere. I'm going to fuck her in every room of this house. I'm going to hide her clothes until we leave. I bury my face between her legs and taste her, salty and sharp, on the plain white fabric.

She moans throatily, then jerks. I look up and meet her blue gaze.

"Dante?" she says sleepily.

"Wake-up call." I pull her underwear down her legs. She helps me, still seemingly not understanding.

When I bury my tongue in her pussy, she gets it. She grabs my hair, pulling me closer, and I have to work to keep enough room between us to lick over her folds. Her taste is overwhelming, so desperately her. I hike both her legs over my shoulders, and she moans. All thoughts of going slowly melt out of my mind. Maybe tomorrow. Or the day after that. Today, I work a hand between us and plunge two fingers inside of her. She rocks into them, smearing her wetness over my face, and I wish like hell I had a third hand to jerk myself off with. There are condoms in a dozen places in this house, including my pants, but I couldn't possibly leave her long enough to get one.

Before long, she is shaking around me, and a gush of wetness spills over my hand. I fuck her through the aftershocks, then pull away to look in her eyes. There it is; the surprise I was looking for combined with the bone-deep desire. She scans my naked body, stops on my painfully hard cock.

"Let me." She reaches out.

"I have a better idea." I wrap my arms around her waist and pull her closer to me on the couch. "I started running a bath upstairs. What do you say you find me a condom, and if you can do it fast enough, I'll fuck you on the way up."

Her eyes grow wide. "And if I can't?"

I smile teasingly. "Well, then I'll make you choose. Do you want as many orgasms as you can take—which I'll decide—or one right before we leave on Thursday."

"We leave on Thursday?" Her grin lights her face.

Something in my chest warms. I want to see her smile like that every day for the rest of my life. I want to cause it.

I back away from the thought quickly. "You have thirty seconds."

She leaps up, heedless of the way her breasts bounce, and I can't fight the smile on my face.

3 4

MICKEY'S

Eleni

ON THURSDAY, I lean back in the passenger's seat and try to see the late-morning sun through the blacked-out windows. Dante's hand rests possessively on my leg, and it feels like an anchor as we drive back into the chaos of the city. After days of his constant touch, I think I might lose my mind if he let me go.

And it doesn't hurt that his hand creeps a little higher at every red light, now that we're off the highway. Desire coils in my gut like he didn't make us late wringing one last orgasm out of me before we left. I don't mind. It was his timetable anyway.

I glance at him. On the ride up, he couldn't stop talking, but never to me. This time, he's been mostly quiet, but he looks at me every time the road doesn't need him. Either way, I haven't learned much.

My stomach grumbles, and I cover it quickly.

"I guess you didn't eat much," Dante says.

We share a smile at the memory of his cock in my mouth before we left. A mile-marker whips by outside the window.

"You're in luck."

155

He pulls into the exit lane and refuses to answer any of my questions until he pulls into the parking lot of a tiny red and chrome diner with a rotating sign that says "Mickey's."

"Now, will you tell me?" I ask.

He smiles. "The house upstate belonged to my parents. My dad used to take me up there for what he called 'guy time' basically whenever he could steal a couple days off, and we always ate at Mickey's on the way home."

I stare up at the '50s relic. It's been almost impossible to get to know Dante, even as he learns every crevice of my body, and stopping here feels just as meaningful as the admission that he cares for me. I climb out of the car, and he leads me inside. Apparently, we choose our own seating and pay at the counter, so he leads me to the back corner booth.

"Did you always sit here?" I ask.

He smiles. "Can you read me that well already?"

I laugh. An older waitress drops off menus and manages to call both of us honey in two sentences. The plastic over the top crinkles and flakes, but the menu is crowded with diner classics.

"How do you pick?" I ask.

He chuckles. "With your heart."

A memory flickers to the front of my mind, and I set the menu down. "Tell me what the best food in this diner is."

"Well, I like—"

I shake my head. "Like that first day. Tell me like that."

The smile that creeps over his lips is achingly fond in a way that makes my heart skip a beat.

"The chocolate-chip pancakes with a side of bacon taste like the first 'guy time' I can remember," he says. "I was, fuck, maybe six, and I only barely knew what the family business was. I scribbled all over the little maze they gave me with crayons while Dad tried to coax me into seeing the pattern. I could tell he was getting frustrated, but we'd just spent a great couple days together, and he didn't want to blow up." He swallowed. "My dad loved me, but he had a temper. Nothing worse than yelling. Still, it scared the shit out of me as a kid. So when the pancakes came, I declared I could do my own syrup, and promptly spilled it all over myself, the booth, and the new toy truck he'd gotten me. Everything seemed to freeze, and I just knew he was gonna start screaming. And I'd ruined the truck!" Dante shakes his head. "The pancakes taste like Dad helping me scrub down the truck in the bathroom and smiling the whole time because he knew how important it was to me."

I blink sudden tears out of my eyes. My chest aches with how much I miss Baba, but I take Dante's hand. He lost someone too.

When the waitress reappears a few moments later, I order the chocolate chip pancakes with a side of bacon, and so does he. We eat in silence for a few minutes. The staff in the kitchen chatter back and forth with each other, an easy mix of work-talk and friendship that doesn't lessen the ache in my chest.

"I didn't want to ask while we were having so much fun," I say, "but am I returning to the city for finals, or for keeps?"

He smiles softly. "For keeps, I suppose."

Relief washes through my body. The last few days have been great, but the days of exile before that were awful. I miss the city. And I can't do anything upstate.

"Cool," I say, trying to seem casual. "Why?"

He sighs and takes my hand over the table. "The...threat that made me move you out of harm's way has passed."

He almost doesn't seem happy about that. A new seriousness covers his brow.

"Okay," I say slowly. "And that threat was...?"

"A non-issue." He turns back to his food.

I frown. "How was it a non-issue? Details would be nice. I like to know who I'm looking over my shoulder for."

He smiles teasingly at me. "Okay. Who are the other major outfits operating around here?"

My face warms. "Other than you?"

He nods.

"The Lombardis," I say. "And, um, I know there are like, quartets in Chinatown?"

He laughs loud and long. I've grown used to his laugh over these past few days. It's a little higher than his speaking voice, like he's pitching himself down the rest of the time, and when he's laughing, he's so comfortable he forgets. I want to bottle the sound and keep it on my shelf at home. Instead, I look out the window, like he can read the thought on my face. He's supposed to be the one possessing me, not the other way around.

"Don't worry about it," he says finally. "I'm the boss. Worrying's my job."

"What's my job in your little outfit, then?" I ask to cover my sudden shyness.

He squeezes my hand. "Your job is to not get kidnapped, not die, and study for your final. I'll have someone escort you to campus as needed, and there'll be guards around the house."

In the wake of the admission that he cares about me, whatever that means to a man like him, it's easier to recognize what sounds like another attempted captivity as protection. Not easy, but easier. I nod and don't complain, at least for now.

We eat until the ache in my chest means I can't take another bite.

"Why are you going through all this trouble?" I ask finally. "The safe houses, the guards."

"Because..." He glances out the window of the diner to the parking lot, a view he's surely seen a hundred times. I can't help wonder what's going on behind his eyes. He shrugs. "Because I would miss you."

My face flames, and I turn to the window as well.

35

DEATH WISH

Eleni

I UNPACK the suitcase I packed so hastily when I left Dante's house into my closet, then pause. This is Dante's house, still, in my mind. And yet this room, this closet, is mine. I shared this bed with Mama. I've cried here, and been furious, and smiled for so long my face hurt. I run my fingers over the pillowcase and look around. Maybe Dante will let me paint this something other than drab tan. Or at least get new sheets.

For now, though, I need to study. I lost three days of study-time to learning everything I could about Dante. Sometime during my absence, someone installed a desk in the previously featureless guest room, which brings another smile to my face. Already, I'm making my mark on this place. I could even be happy here, a ferry ride away from the city. I put my laptop, now thankfully with the Wi-Fi back, on the desk and sit. Daydreaming later. Focusing… now.

"—DO you mean you brought her back?" an unfamiliar man shouts.

I jump, my studying reverie suddenly broken. The sun set while I wasn't paying attention, and my leg aches from how long I've been sitting on it.

"You have…it's been like these last few years!" Dante replies, well above his normal speaking volume, but not so loud I can hear every word.

My heart skips a beat. Dante is fighting with someone. I glance at the closet. I could hide, just let the fight unfold. But it doesn't sound like a rival boss. They're shouting, but they're saying things, not just demanding the other stand down.

"I get out, and…this fucking mess!" the unfamiliar man says.

I slide on a pair of slippers I've taken to wearing around the house, ease the door to my room open, and peer down the hallway. Nothing. They're definitely downstairs.

"I didn't ask you to stick your nose into this fucking mess, Uncle John!" Dante snaps, now much clearer. "You're not even supposed to be out yet."

A family fight, then. Dante can handle this on his own. I start to shut the door again.

"You're damn right I'm not," Uncle John says. "But I heard about this Calimeris girl on this fucking website, and I did the goddamn work to get me out and tell you."

My heart leaps into my throat. They aren't just having a family fight. They're fighting about me. I creep closer to the open wall of the hallway that looks over the foyer below. It sounds like they're in there, and I want to see.

Dante rakes a hand through his dark hair, looking stressed and disheveled. "Yes, fine, I appreciate that."

The man across from him, Uncle John, has salt-and-pepper hair and the same olive skin as all these Italians, but I don't see anything that obviously marks him as Gianna's dad as he shakes his head.

"I keep telling you, Dino, and you're not listening." He takes a step closer to Dante. "You gotta fucking listen."

I mouth the word "Dino" to myself as I sit in front of the railing, lingering over the long "I" in the middle. Surely a childhood nick-name. Any other time, I would've been delighted to have another piece of Dante, but he's clearly angry.

"What do you want me to do?" Dante flings his arms out. "It's a fucking website. I can't exactly raid it and take it down."

"I want you to get out. You're in way too fucking deep." Uncle John shakes his head. "And I don't even know if you can see that."

"What, because Luca Lombardi's come up with a sick new game to lure me out?" Dante's eyebrows shoot up. "Please, tell me why Eleni's picture being posted on some dark web site with a dead or alive bounty makes me in too deep. Because I'm pretty fucking sure all it makes me is about to start hunting this fucking guy."

My mouth falls open. I wedge my slippers between the bars of the railing like that will anchor me here. A bounty? The phrase "dead or alive" shivers over my skin. Luca can't get me in here, right? Do I really trust a few guards enough to take a final with a bounty on my head?

Can I really bear disappointing Baba's spirit if I don't?

"See, that's exactly what the fuck I mean." Uncle John shoves Dante lightly. "You're falling right into his trap! Obviously, he posted about this girl because he knows he can get to you like that. Jesus, Mary, and Joseph, how the fuck did you let him know? How can you not see the mousetrap?"

Dante grits his teeth as he obviously holds back the desire to shove Uncle John. I wrap my hands around the railing to keep myself in place as my own temper flares. I don't know exactly who Uncle John is to Dante, but I know Dante is the boss, and nobody should be able to treat him like that.

"I see it, Uncle John," he says. "I'm not stupid. He's obviously ready for me. So I'm going to start small, find some no-name soldier, and work my way up the fucking ranks until he has nobody to be ready for me with."

Uncle John grabbed Dante's head. "Fucking listen to me. Drop the girl. She's not worth the trouble."

I study Dante. He flinches visibly back, though Uncle John doesn't let go, and he looks like he's been slapped. He looks hurt. Despite all the anger swirling around, my chest warms a little. He doesn't think I'm too much trouble.

Then, he puts his mafia-boss armor back on, and my stomach sinks to my toes. Suddenly, I'm looking at Baba squaring his shoulders as he marches into the living room. Dante cares about me deeply. Maybe even enough to put himself in a lot of danger.

Uncle John shakes his head and releases Dante. "But hey, who the fuck am I? Just the kid brother who got his ass arrested. If you've got a fucking death wish bad enough to want to drive your dad's organization into the ground, more power to you."

Wow. I rock back at the change in energy. My foot slides out of my slipper, and my pulse thunders so loudly in my ears that I can't hear Dante's response, if he says anything, as I grab for it. My fingers graze the edge of the heel and catch.

It drops out of my grip and slaps against the floor below. As one, Dante and Uncle John look from the slipper to me reaching through the railing. My face flames, and I yank my arm back. My second slipper falls in the process, adding insult to injury.

"Come on down and meet my uncle," Dante calls, his voice carefully neutral. "I think you left your slippers in the foyer anyway."

That doesn't do anything to assuage my blush or the guilt churning in my stomach. I try to fix my T-shirt and pad down the stairs. Dante and Uncle John are in hushed conversation when I reach the bottom, and they whip away from each other, both frowning.

"Uncle John, this is Eleni Calimeris," Dante says. "El, this is Uncle John, Gianna's dad."

I smile my customer-service smile as old training snaps into place.

Uncle John steps forward with his hand out. "Calimeris, huh? I think I knew your brother when he played ball with Dino."

I grab his hand to shake. "Yes, we were very proud of Christos."

Uncle John looks back at Dante like this means something. I swallow a frown.

"Well, I'm sorry I disturbed you," Uncle John says. "I'm just out of the clink today, and that never puts a man in the best mood."

"I understand that," I chirp, still shaking his hand. "I mean, I've never been to jail, but I've had some awful bad days."

"Try five years," Uncle John replies.

My smile is frozen on my face. I can't let go of his hand. He maybe broke out of prison to tell Dante I had a bounty on my head.

"It was lovely meeting you, El." He claps his other hand around mine, then pries my fingers off. "I hope you enjoy the rest of the short time you've got in this life."

My stomach drops to my toes.

"And Dino." Uncle John turns to him and just shakes his head. "You inherited your dad's thick fucking skull. Try not to bash it against so much bullshit you break it."

He spins on his heel and marches out through the front door without another word. Dante and I stand in the foyer, feet or miles apart, and stare at each other in painful silence.

3 6

———

IN TOO DEEP

Dante

ELENI TURNS on her heel and marches up the stairs. My chest squeezes, and I race after her. What the fuck was Uncle John thinking? Even if she wasn't here, even if she hadn't overheard, he can't just walk into my goddamn house and talk like I'm still the kid he had to drive to the hospital once because I threw a tennis ball at his garage door so hard that when it bounced back and hit me in the head, I got a concussion. I've been fine on my own for years.

She turns into her room, but she doesn't close the door. A good sign, I think. I follow her in and close it behind me.

A weird feeling tightens my chest further. A couple weeks ago, this was one of many guest rooms. Now the sheets are rumpled, her books are on the desk, and her clothes are in the closet.

Before I can think too much about that, I say, "How much did you overhear?"

She glances at me, and I see tears in her bright blue eyes.

"Okay, so enough." I run a hand through my hair. How do I explain this? Her being posted on one of these sites is a fucking night-

165

mare, but I haven't double-checked Uncle John's information. She could be on some dummy site Luca's goons made sure he saw to light a fire under me.

Or it could be real. The thought kindles some of my rage back up. I have to make sure Eleni's okay, but whether it's a dummy or not, Luca is going to regret fucking with me.

I sit on the corner of her bed and try to gather my thoughts. "Uncle John is old school."

She nods and sits at her desk, her lower lip snagged between her teeth.

"Worse than that, he's been out of the picture since… since a couple months before Frank Lombardi killed my dad," I admit.

She wraps her arms around herself. "So you're still just a…a what? A capo to him?"

God, she's smart. If it wasn't for the way she's holding herself together, I'd grab her and kiss her.

"More or less," I say. "And a capo he met the day said capo was born."

El smiles weakly. "Yeah? Were he and your dad close?"

I knew she was tough, too. I haven't even told her about the potential of a dummy site, and she's already trying to push through her fear. I was right to bring her back to the city. Luca won't lay a finger on her.

"They were about a year apart, so they damn near acted like twins." I smile, remembering the way Dad used to finish Uncle John's sentences, and how Uncle John seemed to have a sixth sense for when Dad was going to need a capo around.

She nods. "And that's why he was yelling at you."

"He was yelling at me because Dad and Uncle John could both be assholes sometimes." I chuckle and rub the back of my neck, hoping to coax a real smile out of her.

Nothing. Fuck. She might actually be scared.

"And because he doesn't realize I've proven myself over these last five years," I say.

Once again, I get nothing but a nod. Should I tell her about the things I've done? The deals I've made, the millions of dollars I've raked in? Or the enemies I've dropped before they got anywhere close to hurting me?

Something tells me the enemy stories would be more comforting to Eleni, but I don't want her to see the same blood packed under my fingernails that I do. And anyway, I know where stories about dropped enemies lead. I can't tell her that. Not now, not ever.

"Luca posted this," I say. "You remember what I said about the dark side of being connected to the mafia? I don't think it's on one of those sites, but it's probably only a couple clicks removed."

She squeezes herself tighter. "I'm sorry."

"No." I'm off the bed before I can blink, on my knees before her, with my hands on her elbows. "You don't need to be sorry. There's a real chance Luca faked the site to scare me—us."

"To scare you," she repeats. "Are you scared?"

I tilt her chin up until I can meet her soft blue eyes, still swimming with emotions.

"No," I say. "Because I know I'm going to do everything in my power to keep him from touching you, and I've been up against worse odds than this."

She stares at me blankly.

I cup her face in one hand. "And because I know how tough you are. I trust you, just like you can trust me. You are safe."

She chuckles, and the smile that lingers on her lips burns down into the core of me like a sip of the best scotch. I pull her into my chest so she can't see my face. What the hell was that?

The rest of the afternoon passes. El and I eat dinner together, late, because she gets caught up in studying again, and she doesn't mention anything about sharing a bed, so I go to my room alone. It's not like we really shared a bed upstate. We only slept next to each other when one or both of us passed out after a round. This makes sense.

Which, of course, is why I'm pacing dents into my carpet while nursing a glass of scotch in the dead of night. I roll my eyes. It's stupid, but I can't stop thinking about that smile I coaxed out of her. It did something different to me, something even the one I watched her share with Seb didn't. I've never felt anything like this before. And it seems like I'm clear-headed, like I'm the same Dante who's led the Saints through trouble as bad as the Lombardis and worse, but part of me wonders if I'm not the best judge of that anymore.

I shoot the rest of the scotch in my glass. The part of me wondering that sounds too much like Uncle John. I just need to go the fuck to bed. Tomorrow, after a night by myself, everything will make more sense.

MY RINGING PHONE stirs me awake. I grab it and answer blindly.

"Yeah?"

"Dante," Tony says, his voice urgent. "You have to get to the port. One of the warehouses just got hit."

3 7

FINAL

Eleni

THE MORNING OF MY FINAL, I pad downstairs in a whirlwind of excitement and nerves. I haven't seen anyone other than Staten Island Saints in weeks, other than the diner. I might be about to pass my first semester of college.

My face is on the dark web with a bounty. I might be about to fail my first semester of college. Around and around again. Hopefully I can block it out long enough to actually pass the test.

I freeze as I round the bend in the stairs. Seb stands there, in casual jeans and a T-shirt for the first time, which I expected. I didn't expect the two other guys in normal, severe suits.

"Did something change?" I ask.

Seb loops his arm through mine. "The big boss figured I'd do better undercover, just another student, so he wanted a set of distant eyes."

I frown. "So something happened."

"Yeah, I finally talked Dante into putting me in a position to get laid while I'm on the job." Seb waggles his eyebrows.

I snort, but I can't shake the feeling he's hiding something from me. Maybe it's just Dante's paranoia after the visit from his uncle, but he seemed okay when he went to bed last night.

Regardless, I let them drive me over the bridge and into the city, all the way to campus. Seb and one of the suited guys get out with me while the third goes to park the car and wait inside, either a getaway or distant eyes.

All my worries about the mafia security team melt away as I re-enter New York City air. It's humid, almost thick enough to cut with a knife, and reeks of garbage. The clamor of a thousand conversations and a million taxi drivers leaning on their horns blot out almost anything else. I take a deep breath and smile. I'm home. And I can crush this final.

Seb agrees to wait in the hallway outside the classroom I have to go to for the proctored exam. I head into the lecture hall. Professor Calhoun hands me a single sheet of paper with a small smile.

"We've missed you, Ms. Calimeris," he says. "I'm happy you could make it today, despite everything–"

"I've missed class, Professor." I cut him off, giving him a forced, but soft, smile. I take the paper and head for one of the desks.

Code a website for a small business of your choice with order functionality using HTML and CSS.

I grin. No problem.

AN HOUR AND A HALF LATER, I hand Professor Calhoun my test paper with the domain name written on it. I designed a website for a fictional version of The Greek Corner, the one I imagined Mama and Baba would've started if they never came to America, called Asteri Mou. Professor Calhoun nods, and I start to leave.

"Hey, wait!" someone calls.

I turn. Another girl in the class, one I've exchanged notes with a couple times, shoves her paper into Professor Calhoun's hands and races up to me. Oh, God, what's her name? Something with an "M," I'm certain.

"Sorry, I get that this is out of the blue, but I'm transferring next semester," she says breathlessly.

"Congratulations." I step out of the classroom, not quite certain what this has to do with me.

"I thought it might be fun to get coffee, exchange information," she says.

No sign of Seb in the hall. He probably took advantage of his disguise to get some girl's number. There's a coffee cart on this floor of the building, the easiest place to flirt with someone very quickly.

"Sure," I say. "The coffee cart down the hall? And then maybe we can sit outside."

She nods, her blonde ponytail bobbing, and I cross my fingers she gives her name to the coffee guy. Actually, if Seb's doing his job and hiding in the shadows nearby, maybe he'll ask for her number, instead.

I smile at the thought.

"I heard about your family's restaurant," she says. "I'm so sorry."

My breath catches. It must have been reported on, but somehow, I didn't think anybody noticed me enough to connect me with The Greek Corner. My project felt like a love letter. This feels like a punch to the gut.

"God, I always put my foot in my mouth," she says. "I totally shouldn't have brought that up. I just felt weird not saying anything, and—I'm shutting up now. How do you think you did on the final?"

"Good," I manage.

She nods. "Yeah, me too. Calhoun's kind of a soft touch, which helps."

I make some agreeable sound and try to scrape my brain cells back together as we round into the atrium with the coffee cart. Voices bounce everywhere, soothing my nerves. By the time we get in line, I'm almost human again.

"Are you transferring to pursue a computer science degree?" I ask.

"Yep." She grins. "My mom wants me in comp engineering, but that's just too dense for me. I basically tap out at CSS."

I laugh, though I don't agree. I'd never considered computer engineering before, but the idea of pushing these skills even further sparks my interest.

We step up to the counter, and she orders first. A non-fat iced latte for Melissa. I was right about her name starting with "M". I hide my celebratory smile as I ask for a black coffee.

"But, I mean, it's hard to knock an engineer's salary," she says as we step off to the side.

"It certainly beats what I was doing before," I reply.

"Customer service?" she asks knowingly.

I glance at her sharply, but she only laughs.

"Come on, no one else hates their job that much. I have horror stories from my time in retail."

I smile, but nerves prickle over my skin. Seb isn't here, either. The crowd is thin enough that I'm reasonably certain I wouldn't have missed him, but I check again, just in case.

My gaze snags on a man who looks...different from the rest. Shinier? He's wearing sunglasses, and he has a cell phone pressed to his ear. Out of pure paranoia, I circle around to Melissa's other side.

His head follows my movements. My stomach drops.

"You know, I just remembered I actually have another class." I start backing away from Melissa. "I have to go."

"Wait, I thought we were gonna—"

"Sorry!" I call over my shoulder as I hurry into the hallway that'll take me most directly to the elevators.

It's quiet, and empty, and my heart rate starts to slow. I'm being ridiculous.

Soft footsteps rasp over the carpet behind me. I spare a glance. It's the cell phone man, but he's not talking on the phone anymore. My heart hammers. If I can just get to the elevator, he can't do anything to me. Those are always crowded.

I whip through turn after turn. I don't care if anyone looks at me weird. But when I reach the elevators, they don't have the line I'm used to when my night class gets out. They're completely empty.

Someone grabs me from behind.

3 8

MOUSE TRAP

Dante

"You're fucking with me, right?" I run a hand through my still sleep-rumpled hair and stare at the foreman of this section of the warehouse.

"N-no, sir." His wide face turns red with the effort of either not yelling at me or not pissing himself.

"Fine. Go away," I spit.

As soon as the foreman disappears, I slam my foot into the nearest crate of goods.

"Goddammit!"

Tony snorts. "I'm glad you're taking the news that we haven't been robbed well."

"Am I supposed to be thrilled someone snuck into one of my most secure warehouses just to knock over a couple boxes of shit and leave?" I demand. "He's fucking taunting me, Tone."

"No shit, Sherlock." My caporegime crosses his arms and leans against a high, metal shelf. "But getting pissed like this just gives him exactly what he wants."

"No," I say with dawning horror. "Racing down here is what he wanted."

"What?" Tony asks, no longer joking.

"Eleni's final was this morning." My skin turns to ice. "And I'm here. I haven't heard from her since I left."

"Shit." Tony sighs. "Okay, where does she—"

My phone rings, and I snatch it up. In that second, I know Uncle John is right. If Luca is on the other end, I'll pay anything, do anything to get El back safe.

"Hey, uh, it's Teo?"

"What?" I frown and check the caller ID. It says Benny's. Why the fuck is Thano's bartender calling me?

"Yeah, I've kinda got a situation here," he says. "Can you haul ass to Benny's?"

"A situation?" I hiss. "Fuck no. You tell me right now if I'm about to walk into a hostage situation."

"Not with us," Teo says.

That icy feeling returns. I hang up and turn to Tony.

"Stay here. Make sure they didn't miss something. I'm going to Benny's, and if I don't text you in an hour, send an army."

***

My car squeals as I slam into a spot in front of the alley that holds Benny's. I'll buy a fucking new one if I have to. I leap out, lock it, and race inside.

In the dim light of the dive bar, three things become immediately obvious. One, no one in this room actively means anyone else ill. I can see everyone's hands and no weapons. Two, the room only holds three people, two of which are Teo and a broad, college-age guy I don't recognize. Three, the third person is Eleni, and she's terrified.

I sprint the rest of the way to her and wrap her in my arms. I know it's stupid, but when she leans into me, shaking, I don't care.

"What happened?" I snap.

Teo nods to the guy I don't know. The guy starts to put his hand out to shake, then seems to notice the way Eleni's clinging to me and shoves his hand in his pocket instead.

"I'm Benicio, but please, call me Ben," he says.

"What happened, Ben?" My voice sounds like it could melt iron. I consider killing this kid if he doesn't get to the point soon.

"Right. So I go to the same college as Eleni, and I saw her show up with this squadron. Clocked them from a couple hundred yards off, and then I recognized her." He swallows. "My dad is one of Mr. Coppola's capos. I recognized her from the, uh, website."

My vision goes red. I dedicate all my brain power to not crushing Eleni in my arms. She doesn't need to hear this.

"Anyway." Ben looks away from me. "I didn't have anything to do, so I figured I'd just keep an eye, see what happened. The first guy in the suit got nabbed when he went for a piss."

I narrow my gaze. "Nabbed?"

"Taken. Kidnapped." He shakes his head. "They looked like Lombardi fucks to me."

My stomach drops to my toes. "And the rest of her…squadron?"

"The one in the T-shirt was led away by a cute girl, then grabbed. I didn't see the one in the car, but it was empty when I walked back outside, so it seems like a safe bet." He shrugs. "So I bolted back inside, called Teo, and got Eleni out of there before anything bad could happen."

Emotions war in violent waves inside me. To have Eleni safe, breathing, in my arms, is nothing short of a miracle. To lose Seb, Vinnie, and Matteo is a blow. Luca got the fucking drop on me. He took me, took everyone off our games.

And he's going to burn for that.

In the silence following Ben's pronouncement, El speaks first.

"They took Seb?"

I turn to her in my arms. Her eyes are swollen, and I can just make out dried tear tracks on her cheeks, but she's no longer shaking. In fact, there's nothing scared in her now. She is a fire, blazing bright, ready to consume anything in its path.

"If he was one of the three, yeah?" Ben says.

"Did you see where they were taken?" I ask.

Ben shakes his head. "I figured getting her out of there was more important."

"They took Seb," Eleni repeats. "Just because I was there. If I hadn't been, he'd be fine."

"It's not your fault." I run a thumb over her cheek.

She shakes her head. There's something going on in her head that I can't quite figure out. But she makes a good fucking point. I need to get Seb back before Tony burns the city down looking for him.

"Teo." I hold my hand out toward the bartender. "Phone. And I want Thano on the other end of the line."

He dials silently and hands me the receiver. After only two rings, Thano picks up.

"Teo? What—"

"Not exactly," I say.

He pauses. "Dante. To what do I owe the pleasure?"

I laugh, anger pulsating through my veins. "I'm done fucking around, Coppola."

"I haven't been fucking around," he replies. "Would you care to tell me why the hell you're calling me with threats from an internal line?"

"One of your capos actually had a decent kid." I glance at Ben. "Pulled Eleni out of a tough situation and brought her here."

He exhales. "Glad it's not a takeover."

I grip the phone tighter. "Hear me when I say this: Luca captured three of my men. I take another blow like that, and it's about to be. Why the fuck haven't you found him yet?"

"These things take time—"

"And you're all out of that," I spit. "If you want a crumb of Lombardi territory, put boots on the ground now and get me a fucking location!"

Thano sighs on the other end of the line. "I like being threatened as much as the next man, but it bears saying. You have what Luca Lombardi wants. Why don't you just lure him out instead of wasting both of our time?"

I look down at Eleni in my arms. She is still burning with that righteous fury. Every moment I have tried to keep her safe, she's fought to put herself right in the middle of things. Maybe it's time to trust her like I said I did. I hang up on Thano Coppola.

"Well?" I say.

She smiles at me, all hunger. "I'm in."

3 9

TAKING THE REINS

Eleni

I SIT on the floor outside Dante's office, listening to Tony bellow inside. Dante warned me this was going to happen. After his call with Thano Coppola, who turned out to be the head of a New Jersey outfit he'd been working with, he took my hands and told me he heard me, he understood, but he needed to tell Tony what happened first.

At the time, that made sense to me. Seb is his brother. I feel sick to my stomach, thinking about his smile in whatever nightmare of a place they've got him in, just because I wanted to take my finals. But I didn't expect the "telling Tony" stage to involve me sitting outside while the two of them figured out what to do, loud enough that I could hear them shouting but not loud enough to make out any specific words. I drop my head back against the wall and try not to groan.

Gianna pokes her head into the hallway and looks from me to the door. "What's going on?"

"They're...Seb...I...." I shake my head, feeling helpless.

"Right." Gianna sits next to me, sipping something dark green.

I raise my eyebrow at it.

"Spinach smoothie," she says.

I grimace. I love spinach—I think any Greek who doesn't might receive the old-fashioned Sparta treatment—but it's not for drinking.

"What, you think I maintain this body eating fried zucchini all the time?" She gestures to her exposed abs. "Pole-dancing is a sport, and it pays better than most outside of the major leagues."

I swallow down a giggle. Dante was right to have her around the house. She has an infectious energy I didn't even realize I missed when I was upstate.

"Seb and a couple other guys got taken by Luca Lombardi," I say. "Because they took me to my final."

"Oh my god, your final was today?"

I frown. "Not really the main thing."

Her face grows serious. "In this life, there's always something. Someone kidnapped, or tortured, or suspected of being a mole. And it all matters. It's life and death shit. But if you let it trample all the normal shit forever, you're going to turn into...well, Dante."

I knock into her shoulder. "Dante's not so bad."

She laughs. "Yeah, you would think that. But seriously. We'll fix the problem in a second. First, how was the final?"

I spill everything about my nerves, about Christos dropping out, about the website I designed and how I think it's good enough but I'm still not certain. And through it all, a part of my mind lingers on the idea that we, Gianna and I, can fix this. Tony and Dante are freaking out. We're talking about grades. Thano said I was the key, so why can't Gianna and I solve the problem?

It's my fault Seb got kidnapped, anyway.

When I finish, I look at her and say, "Do you have any ideas about the kidnapping?"

She glances at the door and lowers her voice. "I'm about to tell you something that, if Dante found out I told you, would get me killed."

My stomach flips. I nod.

"There's a guy who comes into Piacere sometimes who likes me a lot. And"—she glances at the door again—"he's close with someone in the Lombardi outfit."

"Why would that get you killed?" I frown.

She smirks. "Because I'm telling you. And if we... act on this, it might get you killed too."

Something thuds behind the office door. The yelling gets louder.

"Okay," I say. "Let's do it."

DANTE AND TONY left to comb the city for Seb two hours before Gianna's shift at the club even starts, so it's easy to get out of the house. Well, easy-ish. Gianna insisted I had to wear another one of her dresses, which somehow seems even smaller and tighter than the last one. And I'm pretty sure the heels are higher too. But I insisted on choosing my own bag, a little black clutch that appeared in my closet like everything else I seem to own now. I didn't tell Gianna why I picked it, though. I don't want her stopping me.

So, at nearly midnight, an eerie echo of the first time I found myself at Piacere for the auction that changed the trajectory of my life, I totter up to the front door, ignoring the line of people stretching away.

"Hi." Gianna flutters her eyelashes coquettishly at the bouncer.

"You know Mr. Cattaneo guaranteed you access, right, Ms. Cattaneo?" the bouncer asks tiredly as he unclips the velvet rope.

"This is so much more fun!" She blows a kiss at the unamused man and drags me in.

The music pounds into my skull, into the soles of my feet, and I remember a few snippets of my first night drunk. Just a few, though.

Gianna's façade drops. "Okay, I told my friend you were looking for an ex in the Lombardi outfit. Think ditzy airhead who didn't know she was getting involved with the mob."

My eyes go wide. "I-I don't know how to do that."

"What, lie?" Gianna grins. "It's easy."

"Maybe for you." I shake my head and clutch my purse, my insurance policy. "If this plan relies on me lying about who I am, I can't do it."

She takes my hand. "We can just dance, if you prefer. But I thought you wanted to be the badass who saved the day."

I swallow. I really, really do. I want to prove I can. For my family.

"Okay." I nod. "Just…don't leave me alone."

"Done." She nods at one of the tables around the stage. "He's right over there, with the combover."

I grimace at the greasy-looking man with his hand creeping toward his belt as he watches the dancers. Then, I grab a glowing shot from a waiter and plaster on a stupid grin. Gianna leads me over to the table, and I try to tumble into one of the seats like I'm a little drunk. The heels make it easy.

He eyes me from head to toe, arching a brow as his gaze lingers on my breasts.

I wish I could take a shower. I clutch my purse.

Gianna sits on his other side. "This is the friend I told you about, Sean. The one that Lombardi jackass left on read. We're looking for him. Can you work your magic and take us underground, baby?"

"Gigi!" He kisses her on the cheek and slings an arm around her shoulders. "Any friend of Gigi's is a friend of mine." His gaze lingers on my chest again. "Especially when they look like you do."

"So, can you get me in?" I ask.

The man looks me up and down. "I can get you anywhere you want."

I start to get uncomfortable, but then I notice that his arm around Gianna is exposed. A shoulder holster, proudly bearing a pistol. Sean isn't just sleazy. He's dangerous.

"So, when do you ladies want to go? Threesome in the bathroom first?" He leers at me.

It's a good thing I have a gun in my purse.

40

PRICE

Eleni

Sean leers at us through the whole ferry ride and the taxi to the massive club in the city. If I thought Piacere was loud, that's only because I didn't know how loud things could get. I can almost taste the music in here, and people are packed in so tightly I can't remember the last time I took a breath that wasn't mostly someone else's hair. At least it makes walking in the heels easier. There's nowhere to fall.

Gianna clings onto my hand, my only anchor in the storm. I squeeze her and try to seem ditzy when I'm also just trying to think around the crowd.

"So." Sean puts a hand on the small of my back. "Drink first? Bad boyfriend, right? I could treat you better."

I'm about to force myself to laugh when Gianna plucks his hand off.

"She's looking for help, Sean, not a quick fuck."

He grumbles but doesn't seem that mad. I shoot her a grateful look, and she winks at me.

"Are your guys already here?" she asks. "Because if not, she and I are happy to dance for a little while you get that set up."

"Oh, they're here." Sean's mood perks right up. "And thrilled about the delivery, if I do say so myself."

The word delivery shivers down my spine as I remember the website Uncle John came to warn Dante about. Gianna wouldn't have set me up like that, right?

Of course not. I banish the thought.

"Okay. We're ready whenever you are!" I smile brightly.

Sean shakes his head. "No, baby, I secured passage for one."

Gianna's hand in mine tightens. "Just her?"

Sean nods. "Well, me and her."

My heart hammers. I've come this far. I pull out of Gianna's grasp.

"Go dance," I shout over the music. "Based on everything else about him, this won't take very long."

Gianna cackles, but I can see the real worry in her eyes. She doesn't want to send me off alone. But she doesn't know how dangerous I am.

I let Sean lead me out of the club through a side door into a dingy alley. He puts his hand on my waist again, and I try to remove it like Gianna did, but he doesn't move. I swallow.

"Come on, pretty thing, forget this douche," he croons. "Let me show you a good time."

"You know what?" I say, thinking fast. "You're starting to make a lot of sense. But I don't want you to see me get all crazy. So how about you let me handle this douche by myself, and I'll meet you right after?"

He licks his lips, and his gun glints in the streetlights. "I can't wait."

Sean points me up a rickety metal staircase that takes forever to climb in my heels, but eventually, I reach a featureless door. Sean expected me to be ditzy, but these will be real Lombardi men, and I need them to know that I won't be fucked with, as Dante would say. I square my shoulders and knock on the door. A thin piece of wood slides away, and someone's eyes appear behind it.

"I'm Sean's delivery," I say, hating every word.

The wood slides back into place, and the door opens a second later. I march into the small, dark room that sits right above the dance floor, if I had to guess by the thudding base I can feel through my feet. Six men sit within, all relaxed on various pieces of furniture. A haze of cigar smoke hangs in the air, and the room reeks of old alcohol.

Someone slams the door behind me, and I grip my purse. Seven men.

"Delivery, huh?" one of them says. "You're a pretty little present."

The one who shut the door circles around and smacks that guy on the back of the head. "Are you fucking stupid?"

The first guy shakes his head.

"That's what I thought." He crosses his arms and looks me up and down, clearly less inebriated than the rest of the men. "That's Eleni fucking Calimeris."

My heart skips a beat. Stupid. I should've known they'd recognize me. I've walked right into a trap, and I'm going to fail everyone. That same memory of Baba, squaring his shoulders as he faced his death, surfaces in my mind. Maybe I made a mistake. But I have to face it with pride and see if I can't turn it around.

It's what Dante would do.

"You got me." I smile like I expected him to notice all along. "What can I call you?"

"How about a hundred thousand dollars richer?" He grins.

"How about Doll, for short?"

The men snicker. I'm surprised at myself. I didn't expect all those years of listening to Frank Lombardi be awful to my family to ever be useful, but I know the patter of this conversation like

it's inscribed in my blood. In Baba's blood.

He purses his lips. "What do you want? Is this just a death wish? Or did you dress up to try to get a little mercy out of Luca?"

"I want Sebastian Bellini and the associates he was taken with." I cross my arms. "Tonight."

The men all laugh again. The leader, Doll, shakes his head.

"You're cute, but you're not that cute," he says. "I think I'll take the cash."

The anger that ruled me from the moment Baba died rises up in me again. I'm not just here because I want to be the hero. I'm here because there are lives on the line, and that's not funny.

"I'm glad you still think you can get that," I say.

The laughter cuts off abruptly.

"What do you mean?" Doll asks.

"Oh, nothing." I inspect my nails. "Just that you're the first in a line of dominoes that Dante and I are happy to knock over on the way to your boss. Did you really think I was stupid enough to come here alone?"

The playful atmosphere dies. I stay relaxed, reciting the gun rules Dante taught me and remembering the splatter of Frank Lombardi's head. I could kill these men. Any one of them could've killed Christos.

Doll grits his teeth. "What if I can take you to Sebastian?"

"Then I might not have to call in back-up." I grin. "When can we leave?"

Doll steps closer, looking me up and down. "I didn't say I'd do it for free."

The rest of the men start laughing again, slowly and building in volume. My stomach drops to my toes. I might've gotten in over my head. No backing down now.

"Name your price," I say with a smile.

41

———

MISSING

Dante

Tony and I drive back from the city in silence. No sign of Seb yet. We crossed paths with a couple Coppola soldiers, so Thano seems to have finally decided to get his shit together, but that hasn't changed Tony's mood. He sits in the passenger seat next to me, seething. I let him. Now that we're through yelling, he'll start breaking things when it's time to talk again. Right now, all I'll get is sarcasm.

We pull into the driveway, and Tony slams out of the car, but his seatbelt catches in the latch. He rips the door back open, snaps out a knife, and slices the belt to throw it back inside.

"That's going to cost me," I say mildly.

"Seb's funeral is going to fucking cost you." He slams the door again.

I climb out. Tony kicks my garbage can, spilling rotting food onto the lawn I pay handsomely to keep maintained within HOA parameters. An energy drink, one of those stupid fruity things Seb picked up during his brief stint in college, rolls out. He stares at it for a long moment, then sits down on the side of the driveway with a groan. I circle around to sit next to him.

"I called Nonna the other day," he says. "I know we didn't actually have a dinner, but I realized it had been a while. She was furious."

"*Nipote idiota*," I say in my best impression of his nonna. "You think I'm dead already? Ha! Saint Peter himself will have to take me."

He only shakes his head. "She said she hadn't seen Seb in even longer. He forgot to get lunch with her a couple weeks in a row." Tony sucks in a breath. "She asked if he had a new girl, if she should be finally looking forward to a wedding. I didn't have the heart to tell her he was just a little shit."

I stare out at the cul-de-sac I've built my life on. All these days, these years, in this big empty house. Just me, my staff, and my guys coming in and out. It never felt empty until Eleni arrived.

"But he's my little shit," Tony says.

"And we're gonna get him back," I reply. "If he was dead, Luca would be rubbing our faces in it already. He's valuable."

Tony snorts. "Don't underestimate his ability to talk his way into being too much trouble."

"And out of it again." I stand and hold a hand out to Tony. "We've got teams everywhere, and we run this show. Let's go get drunk and tell Seb stories."

"No." Tony takes my hand. "Let's get drunk. But I'm not eulogizing that little shit 'til I see his body."

I laugh as I pull him up, and we head inside. My chief of staff, Andrea, meets us at the door with a frown.

"Is there a problem?" I pull off my shoes. "If not, we're going to be in my office."

"I'm sorry to give you the news, sir," she says. "But Ms. Calimeris and Ms. Cattaneo are gone. I don't know where."

My stomach drops to my toes. Rage boils in my veins. I can't imagine what would make Eleni do something so goddamn stupid.

"Taken or left?" I hiss.

Andrea doesn't wince. That's why I keep her on. "Left, I believe.

Ms. Cattaneo's room shows evidence of a getting-ready process, and the guards report no breach in security."

Luca doesn't have her. Or at least, didn't have her. God only fucking knows what happened when she left here.

"Tell the guards to report to me at shift change. I want to hear this from their own fucking mouths," I say. "And have them start calling around. I want any news."

Andrea nods and leaves. I turn to Tony. My oldest friend, my right hand, stares at me. His brother is missing. Taken because I had him protecting this fucking woman. And now, as soon as I turn my back, she's gone again. The knowledge pulses between us with the silent accusation that I wasted Seb's life.

"What is it about her?" Tony asks quietly.

"I…I don't know," I say honestly.

He grits his teeth and looks away. We have too much history for me to think he'll actually leave me over this, but he's pissed.

"Tell me it's not Christos," he says after a long moment. "Tell me it's her, that there's something I'm not seeing, and I'll fucking figure out how to get right with this. Just as long as it's not you tying yourself in fucking knots."

I'm tired of people asking me about Christos. I'm tired of dreaming about him, as I have since things ignited between El and I upstate.

"It's not about him." I cross my arms. "I swear it on my mother's grave."

He sighs. "Fine. But stop trying to have it both ways, Dante."

"What the fuck do you mean by that?" My heart pounds in my ears, begging me to track down El. I can't leave Tony like this.

"She's your girl, or she isn't." He starts walking away toward my office. "Stop jerking her the fuck around and tell her she is. Maybe then she'll fucking behave. I'll be drunk when you get back."

I blink. I've been holding off on anything official because she doesn't belong in this life. But she keeps choosing it.

Choosing me?

My phone rings, and I snatch it up. "What?"

"Dante, it's Teo."

I exhale sharply. "Tell me you know something about Eleni."

"Thano's got me running ops in the city, so I hear everything."

The pride in his voice makes me see red. I don't crush my phone. Barely.

"So, yes," he says. "One of our best soldiers saw her leaving a club in Manhattan about twenty minutes ago."

"Name of the club," I bark.

"Plush," he says. "But you should know she didn't leave alone. She was with a few Lombardi guys, including one we suspect to be a capo for Luca."

I suck in a breath through my teeth. Rage and panic war. They have her. What the fuck was she doing at a club in the city? If Gianna wanted to go out, she'd go to Piacere.

My skin turns to ice. The two of them would only go to a club in the city if they knew Lombardi men would be there. They don't just have her. They didn't take her. This was premeditated. This was Eleni's plan.

"Just Eleni?" I ask.

"The guy didn't recognize anyone else, if that's what you're asking. Just Eleni and the Lombardi guys, all getting into a car."

So Gianna might not even know. She left El to fend for her-fuck-ing-self, after taking her to that fucking club in the first place. There's no way El knew where to go on her own.

A voice in the back of my brain suggests Gianna might be dead. I shove it away. She has to be alive so I can kill her for this.

I hang up on Teo without another word and shove my shoes back on. I have to get to that fucking club. Everything I need is there. Gianna, or the guys Luca left behind, or whatever breadcrumb trail Eleni tried to leave. I storm out to the car, texting and calling capos as I move. I text Tony last, and he doesn't respond.

As I climb into the car, my phone rings again. The screen in my car flashes the caller ID. An unknown number. I grit my teeth and accept the call as I back out of the driveway.

"Long time, no talk," says a familiar voice.

4 2

PAY UP

Eleni

I TUG the hem of my dress a little farther down my legs and feel the tiny straps strain to hold my chest in. Doll, in the back seat next to me, chuckles.

"Don't bother," he says. "I doubt you'll be needing that dress much soon."

I grit my teeth. He's been saying ominous things like that for the last forty-five minutes, and every time I try to ask him where we're going, he just laughs. I do wish I'd insisted on a longer dress when Gianna and I were getting ready, but nobody's discovered the pistol in my purse yet, so I'm not too worried. Since I'm supposed to be Luca's bride, I think backward mafia logic might save me from sleeping with anybody but him, and if I can get close enough with this gun, I don't even have to worry about that.

Now, I just have to repeat that to myself often enough that I don't panic. Which is a lot, since I'm in this limo with Doll, two of the other men from that upper room, and a driver who hasn't spoken yet.

The smooth asphalt under the wheels turns into something crunchy. Gravel, maybe.

"Almost there." He grins.

"Thanks, Doll." I smirk back at him, and he scowls.

The limo rolls to a stop, and Doll climbs out first, then holds the door open for me. I exit, wobbling over the fine gravel in my sky-high heels. The men just snicker as I struggle. Finally, I catch myself on the hood and straighten to see where I am. The air here is fresher than the city, but not fresh like it was at Dante's safe house. A massive concrete building squats at the end of the drive, and I can see some body of water past it. Maybe a lake? Have we driven so far upstate we've actually reached the lakes?

Doll strides away, and I stumble to catch up. Useless. I need my dignity and I may need speed. I snatch the heels off and hurry after him. He leads me through a side door and into what looks like a back room of a warehouse. A cheap, metal desk sits on one side, and a second door with a window of textured glass blocks my view of the rest of the space.

"Sit tight." Doll leaves through the second door, abandoning me with the other two men.

I glance at the two chairs in the room and decide to take the one behind the desk. Either I have to talk to someone else, and sitting back here will knock them off guard, or he's getting Seb, and where I sit doesn't matter.

The door opens, and in walks someone I haven't seen in a very long time. Luca Lombardi. He has his father's broad build, but small, watery eyes in his wide face, making him look like nothing so much as an overgrown kid. He sneers when he sees me.

"Little Ellie," he says. "I've missed those tits."

Hearing him sends me back to nights being heckled at The Greek Corner, watching Mama and Baba struggle to not say anything. But Frank doesn't own us anymore, and neither does Luca.

"You're going to miss them again soon." I don't bother covering myself from his gaze. Let him look. I know who and what I am. "Where's Sebastian and the other men you kidnapped?"

He taps the gun holstered on his hip thoughtfully. "I don't think I know anyone by that name. Is he one of your little pets? I can kill him before the wedding, don't worry."

I lean back in the chair. "Your man told me I could make a deal for his life. Are we dealing or not?"

"We, as in you and me?" He laughs loud and long. "Ellie, baby, I don't know where you got the idea you have any power here. You're nothing more than a cute little slut for my collection and a way to piss off your master."

I clutch my purse. I'm going to get a chance to show him exactly what I am soon enough. But his hand is on his gun, and there are two other armed men in the room. I can't strike yet. No matter how much hearing him call Dante my master turns my stomach.

"I have already let him in on your little road trip." Luca leans one palm on the desk. "It's funny, I don't actually know which of you is the pet. You both come when called."

The men in the room snicker. Luca smirks at me. No, not at me. At the exposed tops of my breasts. I stand and look him as much in the eyes as I can, wishing I hadn't pulled my heels off.

"I'm here for Sebastian."

He hooks a finger into the front of my dress. "That one is mouthy. Maybe I'll turn him over if you come with me."

I swallow. Only thin straps keep him from exposing me. But this is the opportunity I've been waiting for. "I'll do it. Prove you have him here first, though."

He grins and plucks his finger out of my dress, then knocks on the door he entered through. After a moment, it opens, and someone shoves a handcuffed Sebastian in. My stomach drops. He's covered in bruises, his T-shirt is split, and blood leaks down his face. He lands on his knees with a groan, then peers up at me through the one eye he can open.

"Eleni?" he groans. "You look—"

Luca kicks him in the ribs. "How about an aphrodisiac, my darling?"

I clap my hand to my mouth to keep from screaming as Seb curls into himself. Luca grins and hauls him up by his broken shirt, then sits him in the chair I didn't take.

"Stop, please," I whisper.

"I can't. You see, you were promised to me." Luca slams a punch into Seb's face, splitting his cheek and spilling fresh blood. "And that fucking Staten Island scum took you."

I meet Seb's gaze and mouth "sorry." He offers me a lopsided grin just in time for Luca to punch him again. I wince.

"Dante Cattaneo's taken a lot of shit from me recently." He slams Seb's head into the metal desk, and I jump. "He took my dad. He took my place in the city." Luca grins at me. "He's taken some good fucking men, ones you were acquainted with, if I remember correctly."

"I'll do whatever you want, just stop." I cling to my purse, to the promise of the gun. Luca's so close now, so distracted, but both of the guards are looking at me.

"I have to send a message, darling." Luca kicks Seb off the chair to the floor. "And murdering his caporegime's younger brother is just the first step." He draws his gun.

No one else is going to die for me.

I leap to my feet, pulling my own gun out of my purse, and fumble to get the safety off before Luca can fire.

"Down, boss!" One of the guards launches himself at me.

I squeeze off a shot, but he tackles me, and the bullet goes wide. We land on the concrete floor. The sharp pain of the scrapes on my bare skin contrasts the dull pain of missing my shot. I close my eyes and brace for the crack that ends Seb's life.

Gunfire rattles the air, but farther away. Outside, maybe. Or in the rest of the warehouse.

"Shit," Luca hisses.

The man on top of me climbs off quickly, and I get up just in time to watch him and the other guard hurry Luca out of the side door I came in through. I stuff my gun back in my purse and race around to Seb, groaning on the floor.

The other door to the back room, the one with the glass window, bursts open. I look up.

Dante stands in the doorway, outlined in a cloud of gun smoke. And he looks furious.

4 3

***

MENDING

Eleni

ONCE DANTE and his men cleared the whole warehouse, finding the other two guys Luca kidnapped in equally bad shape, he pulled me aside and told me in no uncertain terms that we were going to the safe house. Apparently we were nearby. I started to argue that I should be patched up at the warehouse with the rest of the men, but the look in Dante's eyes told me it wasn't the time to argue.

So I perch on the edge of the master bathtub we made plentiful use of during our last stay here while Dante rifles through a first-aid kit spread out on the counter.

"Are you injured anywhere other than the scratches?" he asks in the same short, sharp tone he's been using since he found me crouched over Seb.

I can feel the beginnings of a bruise along my side where I hit the ground, but I shake my head. He soaks a cotton pad in isopropyl alcohol and turns to me. Anger still simmers in his gaze. He doesn't warn me before he swipes the pad over the shallow scratches covering my arm. I hiss and try to jerk away, but he holds me in place.

199

"Tell me you're not stupid enough to want an infection on top of this." He keeps cleaning.

The pain burns through me, searing away the last apologies I considered offering.

"I said I wanted to help. To be involved." I glare at him. "And you shut me out again."

"Shut you—" Dante shakes his head. "I went on one search without you. I had a fucking plan, Eleni, if you would've waited a couple hours instead of jetting off to get yourself killed."

"I was fine! I had a gun!"

He scoffs. "I forgot someone nearby getting tackled to the floor while holding a gun is Luca Lombardi's secret weakness. Thank you for saving us all."

I try to yank my arm away again, but he clings to me, iron in his grip. I wince as his fingers press against the developing bruise. His scowl deepens.

"And now you're lying to me. Where else are you hurt?" he demands.

"There's nothing—"

He grabs my chin and forces me to meet his gaze. "I am asking you a direct question. I will decide what I'm able to do about it."

All my frustration boils over. "Why do you always get to decide? Am I actually just a pet for you to boss around? Please tell me, because I'd like to stop pretending that we're anything else."

Something cracks within him, but he turns away before I can read the emotion in his eyes. He releases his hold on my arm and my chin so quickly I almost tumble back into the bathtub. A long moment of silence passes between us.

He turns back with a wide bandage and begins covering my scrapes. "Tomorrow, I want you to leave this place. Don't return to the city. I'll give you a ticket to Greece if you'd like to join your mother, but I want you gone. I'm not facilitating your suicide wish any longer."

I flinch back as if I've been slapped. "That...that's it? Just nice knowing you, get out?"

He doesn't answer.

"I won't stop." I hop off the edge of the bathtub, pulling out of his much softer hold. "You can't keep me out of New York. I'm going to kill Luca Lombardi if it's the last thing I do. I owe it to my family."

He grimaces but still doesn't say anything. My head spins. I want to storm out of here, to leave right now with nothing but the party dress on my back and the gun in my purse. But another part of me screams that I can't lose another person senselessly. I have to know.

"Why?" I ask. "If I ever meant anything to you, just tell me why."

He tenses like I've run a current of electricity through him. "Because you do something to me. You make me into someone... Since I lost my father five years ago, I've been clinging onto a single shred of humanity. Something to keep me above the monsters that run this world. I kill only when I have to, trade mostly in exports. I've kept my hands clean, Eleni. But when I think about you in danger, all of that restraint dissolves." He looks at me, oceans of emotions in his night-black eyes. "I was ready to burn the city to the ground tonight. I was ready to throw this empire my family built away, to let it rot, if it meant seeing you alive again. I was fucking terrified, Eleni."

I'm holding my breath, unable to swallow past a hard lump forming in my throat.

"I have men to worry about. I have their families to worry about. I promised myself I wouldn't do this, wouldn't put myself in a position to lose something so–" he cuts himself off. "I knew what my mom went through being married to a boss. She was always in danger. She was always a target." He runs his fingers through his hair, tripping over his words.

He continues after a beat, "You distract me."

"I'm–I'm sorry–"

"You are constantly in my head," he says, giving me a heated look. "You are the one thing in this world that can bring me to my knees, and the thought of you in danger makes me want to burn everything I've worked for, everything I've built, to the ground."

I stand in silence, my entire body thrumming with nervous energy.

"I can't lose you. I'd rather send you away and never see you again knowing you're safe than find your body," he says softly. He clears his throat. "Fuck, Eleni, I–I love you."

My chest squeezes. That image of Baba pops into my mind again.

"I'm so tired of people who love me dying for me," I whisper.

The corners of his mouth quirk up. "Me too."

I don't know which of us moved first, but I know nothing has ever tasted sweeter than his mouth on mine. He loves me. The knowledge hums through my veins, sings in every brush of his fingers against my bare skin. I am his, and maybe, just maybe, he's mine. We kiss slow and soft, a promise of a better future. I fall into him.

After a long moment, I pull back. "I'm sorry I don't listen well. I spent my whole life being the good daughter, and that didn't get me anywhere. I want to make my own decisions."

He nods. "I get that. And I love that about you. But I need you to listen. Sometimes, it's too important for you to go running off half-cocked. Sometimes that gets people hurt." He hugs me and leans his forehead against mine. "Fuck, El, it scares the shit out of me."

I don't want to scare him. With his arms around my waist and his body pressed to mine, desire starts to curl in my gut.

"Can you teach me?" I ask.

His eyes darken. "How to follow orders?"

I nod and bite my lip.

He releases me and steps back. "Let's start with the lie you told earlier. Since you can't be trusted to tell the truth, I'll have to check you for injuries myself."

I shiver under his incisive gaze. With brusque medical precision, he unzips my dress and pushes it off my shoulders. My breasts bounce free. This dress was too tight for even one of Gianna's bras. But unlike other times, Dante doesn't stare at them. He barely glances. Instead, he picks a pair of medical scissors out of the kit and cuts my panties off. I stand in the bathroom before him, perfectly nude, and wait for his assessment.

He runs soft fingers all across my skin, reporting on my status in low tones. Nothing on my other arm. Nothing on my other leg.

Nothing on my breasts, which he touches with the same distant focus. I shudder, feeling like more than just a plaything for the first time with Dante. It's electric because I know I asked for it, because he's trying to keep me safe. At my lowest with him, I'm his everything.

Dante presses on the dark bruise on my hip, and I gasp at the ache.

"So, you were lying." He clucks his tongue and presses harder. "If you think pain is something you can hide from me, I'll just have to prove you wrong. Get on the bed. Hands and knees, legs spread so I can see your pussy. Wait for me."

He walks out. Disobedience rises up in me, begging me to throw myself at him and try to break this veneer of professionalism. I know what he looks like with his cock in my mouth, splayed naked on the living room couch.

But I don't want to scare him. So I walk into the bedroom and take position on the sheets I already know so well without complaint. I'm ready to listen.

44

OBEDIENCE LESSONS

Eleni

THE COOL AIR whisks over my soaked pussy as I wait for Dante to return. During our last stay upstate, he showed me the wall of toys he keeps in the basement, and we tried out a few. Several of them still scare me, but I can take whatever he gives me tonight. I think.

The door opens and closes behind me.

"Good girl," Dante purrs.

My body sparkles with pleasure, and I sink deeper into the space where I want nothing more than to make him smile.

He swipes a finger between my legs, gathering the wetness there, and I groan.

"Not yet." He circles around to where I can see him. "You haven't earned that."

I shake my head. No, I haven't. But I have earned dragging my gaze over his bare body. He stripped somewhere between the bathroom and here, exposing his taut stomach and the snarl of dark hair around his lengthening cock. I lick my lips. He hasn't abandoned that cool air of command, though.

"Tonight is about following orders and showing you there's no need to hide from me." H e tilts my chin up to meet my gaze. "I always want to know when you're in pain."

I start to melt, to turn back into myself, but he yanks one of my nipples sharply, and I yelp.

"Good." He massages the flesh. "Tonight, I want to hear you. Yell, scream, talk to me, whatever you want. But don't stop."

"Okay," I gasp.

He raises an eyebrow.

I flush. "Okay, sir."

He nods and lays items out on the bedspread in front of me one-by-one. The first, a glittering silver pair of nipple clamps, joined by a chain. One of the toys that scared me. My nipples have always been sensitive. Next, a braided leather flogger. I wince. I know the bite of that from our last time up here. Finally, a blindfold. I glance up at Dante.

"It's very simple, pet. The blindfold is for me."

The endearment shoots straight between my legs, and the evening takes shape before me. I have to prove I can communicate because Dante won't be watching.

"Green, sir," I reply.

He smiles and attaches the nipple clamps. I hiss at the sting, but the ache is what brings tears to my eyes. For him, though, I savor it. I'm listening. Then, he lifts the flogger and puts on the blindfold.

"Fifteen, pet." He runs his hand along my spine as he walks blindly along the bed. "Count for me."

The flogger lands on my ass, hot and sharp.

"One!" I yelp.

The next hit spreads down onto my bare thighs, near the bruise. I rock away from it ever so slightly.

"Two."

Dante pulls me back and lands three more strikes with brutal precision. The burn on my ass blends with the ache in my breasts and melts down into the inferno between my legs. I can be so good for him. He'll see.

"Fifteen," I whimper when the last strike cracks across my skin.

He massages my aching ass. "How do you feel, pet?"

"Green, sir," I reply. I've been so good. I've earned an orgasm.

"No, how do you feel?" He spanks me lightly, setting off a frisson of heat-pain-want.

"G-good," I stutter. "So good. So good for you. Please, sir."

"Please what?" I can hear the smile in his voice.

"Have I been good enough?" I ask.

"For this?" He swipes his fingers between my legs again. "Hm, you're certainly wet enough."

I nod furiously. I need more of his touch.

"I'm going to lay on the bed. Get me a condom. If you can put it on and fuck yourself on my cock while communicating well enough, I might let you come."

"Thank you, sir." I scramble off the bed and grab a condom from the box in his nightstand. By the time I look back, he's already lying flat on the bed, his cock sticking proudly up and his hands pillowed behind his head. I take a moment to marvel at how, even with the blindfold on, he still has total control. I'm his.

I join him on the bed and open the condom, then position it over his tip. "I love doing this for you, sir. I love touching you any way I can." I slide the rubber down. I've never talked like this before, but I'm listening. I'm becoming obedient to him.

He groans, low in his throat. "Good."

I position myself over him. "You're so incredibly sexy just looking at you gets me wet sometimes."

He smiles, and I sink down onto his cock.

"Oh, you feel so good," I moan. "So right, like I was made to fit you."

"Put my hand on that chain between your pretty nipple jewelry." He holds one hand up.

I guide him to the chain, and he tugs, setting off a bright burst of pain that makes me yelp. "Perfect." He smiles. "Don't come until I tell you to."

I begin lifting myself up and dropping back down on his cock, using him like my very own sex toy. Every time I move, the nipple clamps pull on the chain in his hand, breaking up the constant stream of dirty talk pouring out of my mouth with moans and little hurt noises that make him smile. All the time, he just sits there with one hand behind his head and a knowing smile on his face, like he doesn't even need to see me to know what I look like. The smile drives me wild, pushing me to ride him ever faster to coax a new reaction. The disobedient part of me wants to see him come apart. The obedient one wants to earn my orgasm so I can come with him.

He pulls his hand out from behind his head and slides it up my leg to my hip. "I'm close, pet. How do you think you're doing?"

"Good." My voice cracks, ragged and desperate. "Please, tell me I'm doing good, sir."

"I like that." He smiles a little wider. "Beg more."

I balance myself on his chest, scraping against his skin. "Please, please let me come. I want to feel it with you. I want to listen now, I promise, you won't have to punish me again. I'm going to be so, so good."

He squeezes my hip. "We'll see about that. But come for me, pet."

Dante thrusts up into me for the first time, his hips slamming into my clit, and I careen over the edge with a scream. He jerks and stiffens. Then, we both collapse together. I slide his blindfold off.

He kisses my fingertips. "How about a bath and then bed?"

I nod sleepily. I could listen if it was always like that.

4 5

TRACKS

Dante

THE NEXT MORNING, I stir a pan of scrambled eggs—the only breakfast I ever learned how to make on the shitty hot plate I had in my dorm at Wagner—and glance over my shoulder at Eleni. She sits at the island behind me, massaging her cheeks with one hand.

"What are you doing?" I ask.

She blushes just a little and tucks her hand around the cup of coffee she poured herself from the pot she insisted on making first. "Nothing?"

I shake my head. "I thought you were listening now."

Her blush deepens, and she shifts in her seat like she's trying to keep weight off the flogger marks I left on her ass last night. My cock responds instantly. Maybe we'll have a little breakfast to get our strength back and head right back upstairs.

"It's lame but"—she shrugs—"my cheeks hurt because I've been smiling so much."

My chest squeezes. I didn't just have incredible sex last night. No, for the very first time in my life, I told a woman I loved her. And I

209

meant it. She hasn't said it back yet, but I don't need her to. The simple joy in her bright eyes when she looks at me is enough. I've been with enough women to know what I have with her is different. She doesn't have the same experience.

I slide the eggs onto one plate, grab two forks, and join her at the island. "I won't say you're lame if you don't make fun of my cooking too much."

She kisses me on the cheek. "I'm sure it won't be that bad."

I sip my coffee as she takes the first bite and chews thoughtfully. Then, she stands and walks over to my spice cabinet.

"I thought you were sure they wouldn't be that bad," I say.

"They're not."

I laugh at the hesitance in her tone. "Fine, tell me what I did wrong."

She returns to the island with an armful of spices. "They just don't have a lot of depth of flavor. It's just...egg and salt. But if you add a pinch of dill, a sprinkle of marjoram—"

She shakes ingredients I didn't even know I had in my kitchen onto the pile of bright-yellow eggs, samples them, makes a face, and dumps the whole pile back into the pan. By the time my simple breakfast returns to me, it's a crispy omelet with visible herbs poking up through the crust. The whole time, I can't do anything but watch her. She's so goddamn smart, so at ease in my kitchen wearing nothing but her panties and one of my T-shirts. I could spend the rest of my life letting her tell me what to do like this.

"Now, try it," she says.

I lift a bite to my mouth and groan as the flavors spread over my tongue.

"So much better," I say through a full mouth.

She laughs and takes her own bite. "Still missing something, but I think only Mama would know what."

Her gaze drifts away from me, her thoughts obviously overseas. I consider telling her we can bring her mom back as soon as this situation with Luca is settled, but I know where that conversation leads: back to her telling me she wants to be involved in bringing him down.

She needs to make her own decisions. I respect that. But the thought of Luca anywhere near her—

I shake away the thought before I can ruin our morning together by getting so angry I can't see straight and take her hand.

"Last night felt like the beginning of something," I say.

She smiles. "The beginning of my training, I guess."

Tony's words ring in my ears. I shake my head.

"I've been trying to have it both ways." I run my thumb over the back of her hand. "I've been keeping you with me, sleeping with you, parading you around, but I haven't given you the protections usually granted to the…girlfriend of someone in my line of work." I swallow. "Girlfriend or wife."

Eleni looks up at me with some emotion bright in her eyes. "Are you asking me to marry you?"

"No," I say quickly.

Too quickly. Her face falls, and I grimace.

"But that's only because I don't want to scare you off." I cup her cheek and force her to look at me. "And because I want you to be able to get out of this life, if you want to."

My heart pounds. Did I really just tell this woman I could see myself marrying her? The only crazier thing is that it's true. If she said right now, fuck the wait, let's go, I'd jump in the car dressed just like this and head for the courthouse. Maybe I really am losing it. I just can't imagine spending another minute away from her.

She nods slowly. "So, you're asking me to be your girlfriend. Whom you might marry someday."

Suddenly, the fact that she hasn't said she loves me seems vitally important.

"I am," I say.

She meets my gaze. "I'd like that. And I'd like to stay here, with you."

I nearly slump in relief. "Good. Great. Of course, you can stay. You can sleep in my bed."

"If you earn it." She giggles.

I smirk. "Then let's talk about security measures."

"You know how to make a girl swoon," she says wryly.

"This is serious, El." I squeeze her hand to stress my point. "I need you safe."

"And I'm listening." She smiles. "Talk."

I run her through the basic slate of protections. Guards when she goes out on her own. Background checking all of her professors and all the students in her classes. A car of her own with bulletproof glass and a highly encrypted GPS system. A new phone, with a new number. The whole time, she nods along, pausing only to ask that she can give her mom her new number, which I obviously agree to. It's her phone, after all. I only want her to have something not currently Googleable.

"And you'll have to wear a tracker. Some people prefer bracelets or necklaces, but, well, rings have the highest success rate." I duck my head. It's true, but I know how that sounds after my marriage remark.

Eleni goes still, and my heart skips a beat.

"A tracker?" she says.

Thank god. "Yeah, just a simple GPS ping. Only me, Tony, and the head of your security team will have access to the feed."

"A feed. Like live information?" She pulls her hand out of mine. "I'm not a dog you can microchip."

"It's not like that, El." I stuff my hand into my pocket to keep from grabbing hers again. "It's for situations like last night, where you go somewhere I don't know, so I can find you." I stare at the counter and try not to let the panic and rage of finding her at the warehouse overwhelm me. "I can't lose you."

She exhales shakily. "It still feels like the dog thing. But…I'll think about it."

I sweep her up in a kiss.

LATER THAT DAY, I sit in my office when someone knocks on the door. I wasn't expecting a meeting.

"Come in!" I grab the pistol attached to the underside of my desk and cock the hammer.

Uncle John steps in, and I uncock the gun.

"Paranoid?" he says. "Good."

I stand. "What can I do for you?"

"Just came to pass along a message." He runs his fingers along the back of the couch I set in front of the fire. "Somehow, I didn't expect you'd redecorate the office."

"Well, it's been five years," I say. "What's the message?"

"Since the last one went so well," he grumbles. "I wanted to tell you to keep an eye on Thano Coppola."

My heart thuds. "What? What did you hear?"

"Nothing, nothing." He shakes his head. "I'm just trying to keep your head above water, Dino."

"My head is well above the water, and Thano was one of Dad's allies." I eye my uncle, trying to read him. "You wouldn't have turned on him without reason."

"Prison does things to a man." Uncle John shrugs and sticks his hands in his pockets. "Family dinner next week?"

DIAMONDS ARE A GIRL'S WORST ENEMY

Eleni

A FEW DAYS LATER, I'm lazing in front of the TV and wondering when Dante's going to get home. He's been out a lot lately, combing the streets for any sign of Luca. According to him, his plan—which he doesn't want to tell me about yet, in case I think I can do it my own way—works best if he already knows where Luca is. I sigh and change the channel. Without studying to occupy me, I've been alternating between channel-surfing and visiting Seb in the "doctor's office" behind the hair salon a few blocks away. He's getting better, but he broke a few ribs, so the doctor, a nice man who goes by the name Dr. Domino, won't let him go yet. Apparently, my visits are the highlights of his days, because everybody else is too busy to check in. Though he's also dreading getting out because his worried nonna is going to stuff him so full of food that he starts bleeding marinara.

The door opens, and I jump.

"Shit!" I hiss. I don't know when I started cursing, but I have to stop before Mama comes back.

The thought flies out of my mind as Dante leans into the living room doorway. His tie is slightly askew, and I can see a sliver of skin and chest hair.

"Should I be jealous?" I ask.

"Of who?" He frowns.

"Whoever got to tug on your tie." I gesture to his front.

He looks down and smiles sheepishly. "Unless you'd really like to be a low-level drug-runner, I doubt it." He enters the room properly and sits on the couch next to me.

"You got into a fight?" I search him for injuries and find none.

"Barely." He shakes his head. "I knocked his head against the pavement and asked a few questions. The grabbing was him getting back up."

I flick off the TV and cross my arms. "I know I'm safe in here and all, but I wish you'd take me with you. I'm never going to get any better at defending myself if I don't practice."

"You want to practice?" Dante checks his watch. "Let's go practice. The range is still open."

"Not like that." I huff. "When I actually had my shot, I couldn't take it because I didn't know what real shooting was going to be like. My hands were sweaty and shaky and there were people trying to stop me and—"

He cups my face. "El. You don't need that kind of practice."

I tug out of his hold. "Yes, I do! I practice, or I die, right? Wasn't that the point of the whole dating-a-mafioso speech?"

Dating and potentially marrying a mafioso, a voice in the back of my brain adds. I dismiss it. Dante seemed very confident he doesn't want to marry me right now.

"The point of that speech was that you should be careful." He leans back.

"And so should you!" I gesture wildly, just like Baba always did when he got frustrated.

Dante grabs one of my hands. "I didn't come home to fight. I even brought you a present."

That quiets me. My last present was my own set of lingerie, lacy pieces like I see in Gianna's closet, that we broke in that very night.

Even frustrated with Dante, I can't deny how hot he is in his suits. Maybe I even like the suits better when I'm frustrated.

"That's what I thought." He reaches into his pocket and pulls out a long, velvet box.

I accept the box and open it. Inside, glistening on a soft pad, is one of the most beautiful necklaces I've ever seen in my life. A thin golden chain holds a shining diamond about the size of my thumbnail, surrounded by a ring of sapphires, in a simple setting. I lift the pendant and feel something on the back. When I flip it over, the metal is inscribed with a simple message. I love you, El.

Tears sting my eyes. It's the most expensive thing I've ever been given, except for the promised car. It's spectacular. And I still haven't said I love him yet. I don't know what my hesitation is, really. I think I love him. I've certainly never felt this way about anyone before. But there's a voice in the back of my mind that sounds a lot like Mama and keeps reminding me not to fall for the first man who pays attention to me. I don't think Dante is using me. But that voice keeps me too scared to get my heart broken.

"I picked the sapphires to match your eyes," he murmurs.

"It's beautiful." I run my thumb over the back and feel a little more texture. I peer closer and see, nearly hidden under the inscription, what looks like a hatch. "And GPS-enabled."

He winces slightly. "The thing about the sapphires is true."

I shut the box. "I promised to think about it. That means getting to make a decision, not being tricked with luxury jewelry."

Dante cups my hands around the box before I can put it down. "Please, El. I was going to tell you as soon as we got through the tearful, what-a-sweet-present part. You're just smarter than me."

I swallow a smile. "Flattery will get you nowhere."

"It seems like it might get me somewhere." He smirks.

"Nope." I force myself to scowl. I don't doubt he was going to tell me, and I had already mostly decided to wear the tracker, if only to get out of the house more often. But I liked his puppy-dog look. "I'm going to need more."

"You're stunning. Inspiring. I love waking up next to you," he says.

"All good," I incline my head. "But I was thinking something a little more literal."

He blinks at me.

"If I have to wear a tracker"—I open the box again—"you wear one too."

"Easy." He starts pulling the necklace out of the box.

"And I get one of those feeds on my fancy new phone," I say.

He smiles. "Have I spoiled you already?"

"I'm just getting started." I smirk.

He lifts the necklace off the cushion and gestures for me to spin around. "I should've known you'd be trouble."

"Why is that?" I lift my hair.

"You were a brat from the moment I met you." He clasps the jewelry around my neck.

It hangs more heavily than I expected, like a collar tethering me to him, but I don't mind the feeling. I like being attached to Dante.

"I am not," I say through the wash of emotions.

"Oh yeah?" He straightens the necklace and slides his hand down my chest, under the neck of my shirt, to cup one of my breasts.

I nod instead of gasping and lean back against him. He twirls my nipple between two fingers.

"Prove it," he whispers in my ear.

47

SLUT

Eleni

DANTE IS ALL AROUND ME, all over me, even dangling from my neck in the form of this new tracker, and I melt into him. His breath is hot on my neck, and his fingers are hard on my nipple, under my shirt and bra.

"I'm going to stop now," he says, "and we're going to watch some TV. A good girl wouldn't complain. And she certainly wouldn't try to do anything to change my mind. Do you understand?"

I nod. I just have to prove I can resist him. He releases my breast, pulls his hand out of my shirt, and turns on the TV. I glance at him out of the corner of my eye. He's breathing heavily, and his cock already tents his pants a little. Maybe this isn't just about me. Maybe it's a contest of wills. And that, I can win, even if Dante's supposed to be the one in charge.

I glance up at the motionless fan overhead. "It's broken."

"Really?" Dante frowns. "I thought—"

I shake my head before he can get up to check. "Broken. And I'm hot." I pull my shirt off and drop it on the couch next to me, revealing the bra of the other lingerie set Dante bought me, the one we haven't broken in yet. The deep red lace cups my breasts but hides very little.

Dante swallows. "This wouldn't be an attempt to sway me, would it?"

"Never." I shake my head hard enough to make my breasts bounce. "I'm a good girl."

"Of course you are." He sets his hand on my knee and turns back to the TV.

Not enough. But that's okay. He wouldn't be the man I know if he caved that quickly. I stretch out on the couch and, by pure coincidence, my head lands in his lap. He smiles wryly and threads a hand into my hair. The weight is one part comforting, one part deliciously threatening. Like this, he could grab my hair and yank, sending pain sparkling through me, if I tried anything. Still, I nuzzle my cheek against the slight tent of his cock.

His grip on my hair tightens. "Pet?"

"Hm?"

"What are you doing?" He doesn't take his eyes off the show.

"Getting comfortable," I reply innocently.

He doesn't release his grip. But he doesn't move me, either, and I can feel his cock grow harder. He wants a brat. I watch the show, some police procedural, in silence for a while so he starts to let his guard down. Then, I roll over in his lap and look up at him.

"Aren't you hot?" I ask.

He shakes his head.

"I don't believe you. I'm sweltering." I unbutton and shimmy off my shorts, exposing my tiny thong. Dante's mouth watered when he saw this one sitting on the bed, and I understand why. My whole ass is bare, and a slim, high triangle of equally translucent lace covers my pussy. I'm only barely leaving anything to the imagination.

And he seems to be imagining. His cock grows even harder.

"Do you want something?" I tap on the tented pants next to my cheek. "I thought we were stopping."

A low growl tears out of Dante's throat. "No, I don't."

"Good." I nestle back in. "I love this show."

I let a few more minutes pass. Then, I sit up. Dante visibly relaxes next to me. Stupid man. I won't give up that easily.

"I think this bra is hurting my back." I frown, trying to look serious.

He's instantly disengaged from the show, looking at me. "I'm so sorry. Is there anything we can do?"

"Not much." I reach behind me and unfasten the bra. "Just a little massage." As the lace slides away, I reach up to massage my own shoulders. I let my eyes flutter closed and moan at the pressure.

And that's all it takes. Dante crushes his mouth onto mine, trapping me against the couch. I open for him easily, welcoming his tongue. He devours me, and I consume him in turn.

"You little brat," he growls between kisses.

"I didn't do anything," I say with a smile. "You just decided to fuck me."

"You've got one thing right." He meets my gaze, animal hunger in his dark eyes. "I'm going to fuck you like you've never been fucked before, you little tease."

He drops his head to my chest, and a line of bruises blooms in the wake of his mouth. I feel every one, feel the sharp spikes of his teeth against my skin, just hard enough not to break the skin. I moan, loud and long.

Dante slaps one of my breasts. "No. Little sluts like you don't get to enjoy being used."

My breath catches. "Yellow."

He backs off instantly, and I cover my chest with my arms.

"What is it?" he asks.

"That word." I tremble, hearing echoes of every man who's ever thrown it at me for nothing more than existing in my body. "I...I don't like it."

He nods. "I don't have to use it. But know that I think you're gorgeous, and sexy, and you haven't done anything wrong."

"Really?" I looked up at him.

Most of the hunger is gone from his gaze, but it reignites as he looks me over quickly.

"Really." His voice is low. "El, I don't think being a slut is a bad thing at all."

I nod slowly. Some of the hurt starts to drain away. "Even if we weren't at home?"

"Well, I might want you dressed differently if we were surrounded by people." He smiles. "But yes. Always. I want you however you feel sexy, and I don't need to use that word."

I shake my head. "No, you can. I want you to. I don't want it to have power over me."

And I know Dante will never really want to hurt me.

He meets my gaze. "You'll tell me if that changes?"

"Always." I uncover my breasts. "Green, sir."

He flips back on like a switch, pinning me to the couch in an instant. When he drags his teeth over my breasts, I'm caught in his rhythm, instantly back in the moment. Every pinch and swat sings through my veins. I arch up into him.

Dante shoves me back down. "What did I tell you about enjoying yourself?"

"Sluts don't get to, sir," I answer breathlessly.

He pauses for a split second, a breath I never would've noticed when I first started sleeping with him. Now, I recognize it as an opportunity to use my safe words. A moment where I could back out.

I grab his ass. "Please use me, sir."

Dante rips my hand off him and pins it over my head. I squirm in his grasp. He reaches down and unbuttons his pants. His cock springs free, and I feel myself grow even wetter. I open my mouth, let my tongue loll out. He scoffs but repositions until his cock is in front of my face. I lick it, savoring the taste.

"I'm going to fuck your mouth," he says. "And if you're good enough, maybe I'll let you touch your slutty little pussy while you do."

I wrap my lips around him. Unlike when I was learning the ropes, he grabs my hair with a spark of pain and begins thrusting, taking my mouth instead of letting me give it. He hits the back of my throat quickly, and I gag, but I tap the outside of his still-clothed leg, a signal for "green" we came up with for when my mouth is full. Dante doesn't even break his rhythm. He's perfect.

My eyes water, and all my worries begin to melt away. There is nothing but this, us, his necklace bouncing against my bare breasts and his cock in my mouth. It's so easy to roll my tongue over his underside, to groan and feel his balls tighten in response.

"Touch yourself," he hisses.

I slide a hand in between my legs and find the tiny red underwear soaked through. I shove them aside. Finding my clit is second nature now. Circling it in rhythm with his thrusts is as easy as breathing. I stuff my other hand down there and curl two fingers into myself in the same rhythm, like he's fucking me everywhere.

He thrusts into me once, twice, three times more and comes with a moan. I swallow quickly, but some still escapes, dribbling onto my bare breasts. He starts to withdraw, and my heart skips a beat. I'm so close. He won't leave me hanging now, will he?

Of course not. Dante leans back and watches me fuck myself with hungry eyes. "Such a good little slut."

I am his slut. And he loves me. I come with his name on my lips.

4 8

ET TU?

Dante

"WHAT DO YOU THINK?" Eleni twirls, showing off the suit she picked out for the occasion.

I smile from my spot on her bed. "Perfect."

And it is. I figured, since we couldn't do anything real about Luca yet, El could be let in on a little of the planning. After the necklace, and our rendezvous on the couch, it was harder to forget how strong she was. And she threatened to start following me in the car I bought her. So I set up a face-to-face with Thano to get them officially acquainted, and Eleni went online shopping in secret, leading to the all-black suit she's sporting now. She's obviously teasing me, but she looks fucking incredible. The knee-length skirt fit her like a glove, and she's swapped out the tie I would wear for some tight, black necklace that highlights the line of her throat. She's pulled her hair up in a bun, leaving only a few curls loose to frame her face, and the heels she's wearing would put Gianna to shame, albeit not on a work night.

"You think?" She fidgets with her coat. "I feel like I look silly. And the buttons on the shirt pull—"

"Don't remind me." I stand and wrap her in a hug. "Next time, I'll get you a tailor. Though we're keeping this shirt to rip off you."

She presses herself against me. "How long do we have?"

I check my watch. "Not nearly long enough. We have to fight Verrazano traffic at rush hour. I swear, Thano's a sadist."

"Takes one to know one." She pinches my ass.

I swat her away with a smile, and we walk outside hand-in-hand. The drive in is, predictably, torturous.

"So, Thano—I can call him Thano, right?" she asks.

I smile. "Yes, you can. You're high enough in my organization."

That makes her glow bright enough that I almost don't want to kill everyone on the bridge.

"Thano leads a syndicate in New Jersey." She plays with her new necklace. "So why are you working with him?"

"We have some shared interests." I lean on the horn as someone tries to cut me off in bumper-to-bumper traffic. "Both of us would love a slice of New York City. And he's got more men, mostly because he has more room to spread out."

She nods. "So, you're allies."

"For now." Blessedly, I pull off the Verrazano and into regular New York traffic. "Alliances in this business don't tend to last."

Uncle John's warning echoes in my ears, but I ignore it. He's just second-guessing my every decision. I don't need him.

"Is this like your equivalent of a work party?" She smiles.

I laugh. "If that's an easy way for you to think of it, then yes. There will definitely be drinks, and maybe food."

"That, I can handle." She nods to herself.

"I'm pretty sure you can handle anything, El."

Forty fucking minutes later, we pull up outside of Benny's, and I open the glove box.

"First, phones in." I throw mine inside. "It's a respect thing."

She follows suit.

"Then, one for me"—I pull out my favorite pistol and slide it into my shoulder holster—"and one for you." I offer her a silver gun with scrolling detail work I picked up recently.

"Heck of a work party." She takes the gun delicately and holsters it on her waist.

"Welcome to the business." I climb out of the car, then help her out, and we walk inside.

Teo waves us immediately through the curtain to the back, and El clings to my hand as the dive abruptly transforms from hole-in-the-wall to Fortune 500. Thano likes everything black and chrome, and his city headquarters is no different. We sit in a small waiting area, where she taps her feet like she had six cups of coffee before we left, and then the door to Thano's office opens.

He smiles warmly. His iron-gray hair is tied back in a ponytail, and the years line his face. "Good to see you, Dante."

El stands and sticks out her hand. "My name is Eleni Calimeris and I'm his girlfriend."

"Nice to finally meet you in the flesh." Thano chuckles and shakes her hand. "Please, come in."

I stand. "This is really just an introductory meeting. You said we were closing in on Luca, right?'

"Yes, I picked up a significant lead on that warehouse upstate." Thano walks into his office.

El and I trail after him. As predicted, his drink cart sits in the middle of the room, and a small tray of antipasti perches on a small table between the two black armchairs in front of his desk. I take a seat, and the back of my neck prickles. Thano didn't have those red curtains on his window the last time I was here.

"You redecorating?" I ask.

He follows my gaze to the curtains. "Oh, that. My wife said I was getting dreary, refused to come into the city unless I did something in here."

Paranoia. I chuckle and gesture for El to sit. "She was right. It was downright funeral here."

He smiles tightly. "Something to drink?"

"Scotch," I say.

"Wine. Rose, if you have it." El smiles.

I raise an eyebrow at her. She still doesn't drink often.

As Thano pours the drinks, she mouths "Gianna," and I smile. Of course. My cousin has been corrupting her.

Thano raises his own glass, full of something clear. "To a long and healthy partnership."

"Cheers." I raise mine.

Something rustles. The back of my neck prickles again. Thano's gaze darts to the side, toward those goddamned curtains, and I realize a moment too late that I sat Eleni between me and them. Two men explode out of the drapes.

I grab for my gun. Stupid. One of the men lunges for Eleni and snatches her around the waist while the other rips the curtains off the wall and throws them at me. My vision goes red, and not just with anger.

"Dante!" Eleni shrieks.

Glass shatters. I rip the knife I barely use out of my inside jacket pocket and slice through the curtain, but it's already too late. The goons smashed through a fucking window. I race to the sill, heedless of whatever Thano is up to, just in time to watch them throw a still-struggling Eleni into the back of a white van and take off.

The anger that washes through me grants clarity. This whole city will burn. Shooting them would be a waste of bullets. I'll taste their blood when I find Eleni. I whip back to Thano, who still stands behind his desk with his glass raised, though he's lifted his own gun.

"How long?" I ask.

He finishes his glass. "Didn't I tell you? The lead I found at the warehouse was a charming young man with an interesting proposition by the name of—"

I fire. Clean shot, right between the eyes. He can monologue to Saint fucking Peter. Thano Coppola was just the first obstacle in my path.

By the time I make it back to the front of Benny's my suit pants are drenched in blood, and the Coppola organization has at least a dozen positions to fill; including boss. I storm to my car, yank open the door, and rip my phone out of the glovebox. Eleni's clatters to the floor, and the sharp, clear anger is all that keeps me from breaking down. I dial Tony with steady hands.

"How'd the meeting go?" he asks.

"Gather a hunting party," I reply.

4 9

FAMILY TIES

Eleni

I BLINK awake to an ache in the back of my head so intense that, for a moment, I expect to see a cheap couch and smell gas like I did in the basement of Frank Lombardi's garage. But the surface underneath me is cheap vinyl, like a couch from the fifties, and I smell…salt? I run my hand over the back of my head and find a huge bump.

Wait, I run my hand over my head? I'm not restrained. For a split second, I let myself hope I missed the fight while unconscious, that I'm already in some new safe house of Dante's. I open my eyes a crack and peek around.

No such luck. Men with guns parade through the warehouse around me. I lay on exactly the sort of couch I was picturing, which happens to be blue, against one wall. Most of the men wear T-shirts from the garage and barely ever stop touching their guns. My heart pounds. Luca has me. He…what, convinced Thano to turn on Dante? The mafia politics are too hard to follow with my head pounding louder than the drums in the Thanksgiving Day parade.

As I watch, one of the guards nudges another and looks at me. The

231

second one nods and walks away. Damn it. They realized I'm awake. I close my eyes and try to stretch out on the couch like that was a brief blink of consciousness while secretly checking for the gun I brought into Thano's. No luck. All my pockets are empty.

My heart leaps. My pockets might be empty, but my necklace is still on!

Footsteps lumber up to me and stop.

"It's cute that you think you can trick me, Ellie," Luca says. "Or do you just want our first time not to be your fault? Your ass is tempting, up in the air like that."

Anger flushes my veins. He killed Christos. He may as well have killed Baba. He's the reason Mama left. I won't let him get the better of me again.

I sit upright and fix my skirt over my knees. "It's cute that you think you can rattle me by objectifying me."

"Cute?" He makes a face at the man next to him, the guard who seemingly left the room to get him. "She thinks I'm cute."

That man laughs. Luca backhands him.

"Look at what you make me do." He grabs my chin and forces me to look at the man as a bruise forms on his cheek. "Val, get out of here before I have to castrate you to impress her."

The guard nods and scurries away, leaving me with Luca. As much as we can be left in an empty warehouse.

"What do you want from me?" I demand.

"I want you to learn your fucking place." Luca backhands me.

Pain sparks through my vision, and I tumble to my side on the couch. How did the guard stay standing? All my teeth feel loose.

"That means"—he hauls me to my feet by the lapel of my jacket—"you stop playing mafiosa and start playing docile housewife."

Rage courses through me. I've never been closer to him. "Okay."

He blinks. I lean in like I'm going for the kiss. He leers at me.

I sink my teeth into his lower lip with all the force I can muster. He rips himself back from me with a yell, and a piece of his flesh remains in my mouth. I spit it out before the taste of blood can overwhelm me and try to remember everything I know about fighting hand to hand.

Luca whips out his gun and presses it against my throat. I freeze.

"You little bitch," he hisses. "I'll end it right now. I'll fuck your corpse just as happily and toss it out to your fucking master still full of my cum."

I swallow. The metal freezes my skin.

"That's what the fuck I thought." He bashes the gun against my head.

I stumble and catch myself against a shelf. In seconds, the gun is against the back of my head. I can't move. I've failed everyone.

Luca traces a finger over my shoulder, then rips my jacket off with a sound of tearing fabric. I wince. He presses the gun against me harder, crushing my face into the metal shelf, daring me to say anything as he reaches around my front and tears my blouse open, displaying my bra for all to see.

"Move." He pulls me away from the shelf and shoves me forward.

I stumble ahead of him on numb legs. Everywhere I look, a new man is leering at my chest, laughing with his friends, saying something crude. All of them are armed.

But Dante's necklace bounces between my breasts. His voice echoes in my mind, and being seen like this is less shameful. I have nothing to be ashamed of. These men do.

Luca shoves me into a side room. "My men like the show, but I can tell you perform better in private."

I turn to him and open my mouth to retort, but he shoves the gun inside. I gag as he steps closer, shoving the weapon further down my throat.

"Think really hard about what you're going to say next, Ellie," he murmurs. "You're not the only Calimeris I know how to reach."

I blanch. Mama, he knows about Mama.

"Now you're getting it." He pats my cheek so hard they feel like small slaps.

My eyes water. If he knows about Mama, the GPS necklace

doesn't mean anything. I'm not just running out the clock anymore, I'm doing whatever I must to stop him from going after her.

He pulls the gun out of my mouth, its barrel now slick with my spit, and nods. "I know a few things about your big brother too. But I have a sense you're not ready for those yet. I'll break you in a little first."

My mouth falls open. He's taunting me about killing Christos, promising details. Maybe the location of his body. Maybe awful things I'd never want to know.

"God, you really are prettier when you're not talking." He slams his fist into my gut.

All the air leaves me in one gust, and I crumple to the floor.

"By the time I come back, I want you better behaved." He spits blood on me, then steps on my hand, sending pain lancing up my arm. "If you're feeling strong enough, maybe strip for me. I know the guys would really like that."

I swallow down the insults I want to scream at him and let him close the door and walk out. When I curl into myself, crying as quietly as I can manage, the air around me reeks of blood.

5 0

ONE NIGHT STAND

Eleni

THE DOOR SLAMS OPEN, and I startle out of the fetal position I've been curled in since Luca left. I haven't even buttoned my blouse.

Luca sighs. "Well, I was really hoping to get a look at that pussy of yours, but your tits will have to do."

I stare up at him blankly. Don't say anything that could hurt Mama. He sneers at me, his lower lip still matted with blood. The rage I'm tamping down flares gleefully when I see that.

He rolls his eyes and hauls me to my feet by one arm. Thankfully, he doesn't grab the one attached to the hand he stepped on. Small miracles.

The men whistle and leer as he leads me through the warehouse again, to a different section. I keep my gaze on the ground as much as I can. For Mama's sake, I do not memorize these men's faces so I could destroy them later. I know how to behave.

But when Luca leads me to a clearing in the high shelves, and I see Dante, Tony, and a bruised Seb, everything else falls away. He found me, just like I knew he would. And he's safe. New scrapes mar his

235

knuckles, and a spatter of blood that doesn't seem to be his stains his cheek, but he's safe. If I can tell him Luca knows about Mama, I can save the two of them at least.

I meet Dante's gaze and find it nearly feral with fury. The moment slams back into place. I am bruised, maybe bloody, and half-dressed in Luca's hands. Dante won't listen to a word I say until Luca is dead or dying. I try to catch Seb's eye instead, but he seems dedicated to not looking at my exposed body. I'll appreciate that later. I need him now.

Luca throws me onto the floor, and I catch myself on my hands and knees. A low noise tears out of Dante's throat.

"So much trouble for such a little scrap of meat." Luca drags something hard over my back, my ass. I don't need to look to know he's pulled out his gun again.

"Let her go," Dante growls.

Luca laughs delightedly. "Ooh, she isn't just an afternoon delight, is she?"

I sit back on my heels and look up at Dante. The fury in his face is a living thing, worse than I've ever seen before. He's on the verge of doing something awful.

"And she kneels!" Luca crows. "Got her trained up already, I see. Well, in that case, I have a proposition."

I mouth the word "Mama" to Seb. He's still not looking at me. My heart pounds.

Luca drags his gun over my shoulder, down my chest, until I can feel the cool metal on the tops of my breasts. I don't flinch. I won't give him the satisfaction. Dante fights to regain his cool, likely for the same reason, but I watch it fray at the edges.

"You took something that didn't belong to you," Luca says. He tilts my chin up with the barrel of the gun. "Her ass was already promised to me by her sainted father."

I nearly forget about Mama as the same true, deep fury in Dante washes over me. Baba did not sell me. He died so he didn't have to. He died to save me. I open my mouth—

And quickly shut it as Luca plays the gun over my lower lip. I won't give him the chance to take advantage of me again.

"But I'm a generous man." He slides the gun back down and pushes my bra strap off my shoulder. Luckily, the cup has its own stability, so I'm not exposed. "I'll take one night."

Dante pulls out his own gun and holds it tight in one hand. I watch Tony brush against his shoulder, clearly a silent temper check.

"If you agree"—Luca runs the gun under the cup of my bra until I can feel the cool metal on my nipple—"I'll be happy to give her back to you in one piece and leave you alone."

"I'll do it," I say. Alone means he won't touch Mama.

Dante's face goes purple.

Luca tuts. "You remember the talk we had about your place, Ellie?" He rubs the gun up and down between my breasts. "You're his, so I'm talking to him. Nobody cares what you think." Luca chuckles. "And if you knew what I know about Dante Cattaneo, you might not be so quick to throw yourself on the flames."

I glance at Dante, wondering what Luca is talking about. He doesn't look at me with a strained dedication that tells me not looking at me is the only thing letting him keep his cool.

"And let me guess," Dante says stiffly, "that means you want to hear me say it."

"Ding, ding, ding." I can hear the smile in Luca's voice. "I want you to hand your girl over to me because it's what I'm owed, and I want you to know you don't have another choice." He threads his fingers into my hair.

For Mama, I do not shake him off. For Dante, I sit there tall and proud, like I'm just as polished as I was when we left to meet Thano Coppola. Luca can take the lives of so many I've loved from me, but he can't take my pride. One night with him would be a nightmare, but no worse than what I expected when I signed up for the virginity auction. I can handle this.

Dante looks at me for a long moment. I try to beam my warning about Mama into his brain, and my certainty that this is the only way out. If I am a pawn to Luca, fine. Let him take me into his bed and regret it for the rest of his days. I can bite more than his lip.

"One more thing." Luca's hand in my hair tightens. "I want your word that when she decides to leave you for me, you'll give us the same courtesy and stay away."

Dante laughs, though it's a choked sound. "You really think she'd choose you?"

"I really think I know the right words to convince her you're not the man for her." Luca's words drip with meaning I don't understand. "Oh, she's so much prettier when she's scared."

Dante fires.

FIRESTORM

Dante

MY BULLET PINGS off a metal shelf as Luca Lombardi ducks at the last moment, dragging El down with him. She yelps and tries to disentangle his fingers from her hair. My vision narrows to her, half-dressed on this filthy warehouse floor. She looks so vulnerable, nothing like the iron woman who tried to stand up to him moments ago. How dare he expose her like that, how dare he grope her with his fucking gun like a piece of meat, how dare he threaten—

Tony drags me down behind a table I didn't realize he flipped over for cover. "Head in the game, asshole."

"Fuck off." I reload my gun. I don't want to miss my shot on Luca because I emptied a chamber into a fucking shelf.

Tony slams me against the table. "Head in the game, or I'm dragging your ass outside and chaining you to the car until it's over."

I grit my teeth and try to swallow down enough of the white-hot anger that filled me and made me fire that first shot. I can't save El if I'm dead. There's no life to share with her if I don't have one. Tony releases me and nods. I peek up over the top of the table to see Luca's men hiding in crevices amidst the shelves. Fuckers. This is Thano's fucking warehouse in Jersey. There's no reason for them to know the place so well already.

"Whack-a-mole," Tony hisses.

I nod and disappear back behind the table. Tony pops his head out like he's not paying attention. When Luca's men expose themselves trying to get the shot, I shoot one, two, three of them in quick succession. They drop, and Tony hides himself again.

"Me next," I spit.

Tony grits his teeth but doesn't refuse me. I need to see where El is. I lean out, perfectly unconcerned.

Luca's gone. Luca's fucking gone, and he took her with him. Tony's gun fires next to me, but I don't duck back down. I whip around, trying to find her.

There, by the open loading dock. Luca still has her by the fucking hair, and he's dragging her—

Tony yanks me back down hard enough that my head slams into the table. "Are you fucking stupid?"

"He's going for the loading dock." I shove more bullets into my gun. "We have to move."

Tony mutters something that sounds suspiciously like, Uncle John was right, and nods around the table toward the loading dock. I'll tear him a new one for that later. There was a whole fucking fleet of identical black cars in the parking lot when we pulled in, after chasing the tracker all the way to the Jersey fucking Shore, and I'm not losing El in one of those. Luca will find the tracker before long.

Tony and I dodge to a nearby shelf. Bullets fly. Someone grunts, and I glance into the next row over to see Seb and one of Luca's men, fighting hand to hand on the ground. I take aim and splatter his enemy's head.

Seb looks up at me and wipes gore off his face. "Thanks."

"Figured I owed you." I nod at the loading dock. "El that way."

The three of us prowl forward, dodging bullets and sprinting between the thick cover of the shelves. Every time I drop one of Luca's men, I duck behind Tony and reload. I won't miss. I can't miss. It's just barely easier to think straight when I can't see El, her breasts barely contained by a black lace bra she must've bought at the same time of the suit, covered in bruises and refusing to break under Luca's force.

We reach the edge of the shelves. Only floor between us and the loading dock. Floor, and seven of Luca's goons. Behind them, I can see Eleni struggling, can just barely hear the tirade she's unleashing against Luca as he drags her through the gravel. That white-hot anger fills me again.

A crowbar sits on top of one of the crates next to me. I pick it up and throw it in the opposite direction of Seb. When the guards turn to follow the noise, Tony and I charge. My gun judders back and forth in my hand, barely a breath between when I fire one bullet and when I sight my next shot. In the head, in the chest, in the stomach so I can interrogate him later. One of them clips my shoulder, a searing flesh wound. Tony takes him down a second later.

And with all the attention on us, Seb has all the time he needs to creep past the guard and fire on Luca. His gun's distinctive, raspy fire cuts through the fighting to me. Tony drops the last guard here, though gunfire deeper in the warehouse tells me the rest of our men are still fighting. I whip around to check on Luca and El.

Seb's first shot went uselessly wide. His aim still isn't what it used to be, even on the edge of the loading dock in perfect form. Luca opens a black SUV. Seb's next shot shatters the window of the door Luca is holding. The big fucking coward dives into the car, releasing Eleni's hair. My chest squeezes.

El scrambles to her feet in the gravel and begins racing toward me. I drop my gun and run for her. She's here, she's safe, she's mine. I'll move her out of the city, to fucking Greece, wherever she wants, as long as I never have to see her within a hundred feet of Luca Lombardi again. My grasp on the monster inside of me is slipping. It's almost hard to run to her instead of throwing myself at the SUV to gut Luca and feed him his own entrails. As long as she's safe, I can be the man she cares about.

Like a monster out of a movie, Luca rises up behind her. He lifts his gun. I throw myself forward, and he fires.

5 2

I LOVE YOU

Eleni

THE WORLD SLOWS AROUND ME. Gravel crunches under my bare feet. Oh, god, how has this happened? Everything hurts as I sprint across the warehouse parking lot to where Dante fell.

Gouts of crimson blood stains the rocks in front of him. My heart hammers, drowning out voices and gunfire and anything else. I drop to my knees and skid the rest of the distance, barely noticing the pain as my skin shreds. His eyelids flutter. Not dead. Yet.

"Eleni." He reaches for me with a weak smile.

My heart is in my throat. I run my hands over his chest, not bothering to be careful, until I find a patch of his suit soaked through with blood. Right in the middle of his chest. Tears fill my eyes, magnifying the shine on something a bit behind him.

His gun.

Luca begins laughing. "Looks like we've got more than one night to enjoy, Ellie."

My feet move before I know what's going on. All I know is that

Luca has taken too much from me. I'm tired of hiding, of waiting, of preparing. I snatch Dante's gun out of the gravel.

Finger on the trigger. Roll it back. I have never wanted someone dead more than Luca Lombardi. The gun, still warm from Dante's hands, jumps, and Luca falls. Tears stream down my cheeks. I pull the trigger again and again, but it only clicks. Dante had one bullet left.

Someone puts a hand on my shoulder, and I jump. It's just Tony. He looks at me with nothing but worry in his eyes.

"Seb's calling Domino," he says.

Dante. I toss the gun aside. Having Luca dead doesn't mean anything to me when Dante's bleeding out. My weeks of hunting revenge fizzle away as I scramble back to Dante's side.

"El," he mumbles.

"I'm here." I take his blood-soaked hand and clutch it to my chest.

"It was a small-caliber bullet," Tony says. "That's good news."

I can barely listen to him. Every sense I have attunes to Dante, the rasp of his breathing and the tremble of his hand in mine.

"This is why I wear black," he says.

I force myself to smile through my tears. "Why?"

"So no one can see the blo—" He coughs as Tony leans on his chest.

"What are you doing?" I yell at Tony. "Get off!"

"You want him dead?" There's no humor in Tony's face. "I'll get off if you want him dead."

The words land like stones between us. Dead. Dante is dying. He'll die if we don't move fast enough. Oh, god. The smell of blood surrounds me, and it's like I'm in the apartment again, realizing Baba is dead because I landed in his blood on the carpet. I press a hand to my mouth. I can't lose Dante. Luca can't take someone else I love from me.

"I love you," I gasp before I can lose my nerve. He has to hear it if… if this is my last chance.

I don't know what to expect. Another smile, maybe. A feeble kiss. Maybe even a snarky look from Tony to undercut the moment.

What I don't expect is for Dante to go pale and whisper, "Don't say that."

"What?" I ask.

He shakes his head. "Don't—you can't—"

I cup his face. "I do. I love you. Tell me what's going on."

He closes his eyes like he's gathering strength for something. Seb skids up, sending gravel flying.

"Domino's too far out. He's sending a colleague."

Tony nods. I don't look away from Dante. Finally, he opens his dark eyes again.

"Luca wasn't wrong," Dante says.

My stomach sinks. He's delirious and we're losing him.

"Listen—" He coughs again, and I watch droplets of blood spatter out of his mouth, onto Tony's sleeve.

Whatever he has to say now, it's fine. I love him. There's nothing he can say to stop that.

"I know what happened to Christos," he says finally.

I squeeze his hand. "We can talk about this later."

If there is a later. A life I didn't realize I'd dreamed up for us flashes before my eyes. Dante and I gathering Mama from Greece, installing her in the house on Staten Island with us. She'd open her own restaurant out there, though she'd have to get new help. I'd design her new website and finish getting my degree while working side-by-side with Dante to run New York City better than Frank Lombardi could've ever dreamed. We'd put Baba and Christos to rest, for real, and start to heal as much as we could. Maybe we'd even bury them alongside Dante's parents so Baba could meet them in the hereafter.

Dante squeezes back, a hollow ghost of his normal strength, and I snap back into the moment.

"You're not listening," he says. "El, Christos ran with the Lombardis."

I shake my head. "Mama thought he might've started hanging out with them, but he wasn't actually a member of their organization. He wouldn't have."

"He did." Dante groans. "And… and I hate the Lombardis."

I frown. None of this makes any sense. What is he saying? Why is he wasting our last moments talking about this?

Tony shakes his head. "You shouldn't do this now. She loves you, you're going to live. Let that be enough."

"Can't have it both ways." Dante smiles weakly. "I hunted down a group of their soldiers. Tortured them for information, killed them."

That's his job. I don't understand.

"I killed Christos."

I lean back, the world going slow again. A car pulls up with a spray of gravel, and a woman with a doctor's bag climbs out. Tony seems to explain the situation, then climbs off of Dante. I am pushed back— pulled back by someone. Warm hands. I don't know who. Dante killed Christos? That's just not—I mean, it can't—I can't have—

My pulse roars in my ears. The doctor crouches over Dante, doing something. Everyone looks severe. I just keep staring at Dante as his eyes flutter closed. He killed Christos.

It turns out he could say something that might stop me from loving him.

Keep reading! Chapter 1 of *Loved by the Mafia King: Mafia King's Book 2* starts now!

LOVED BY THE MAFIA KING
CHAPTER 1: A HUGE MESS TO CLEAN UP

Eleni

I stare out of the wide window in the bedroom I used to share with Mama over the Narrows. The setting sun glints off the water, and my heartbeat pounds slowly in my ears. I don't remember coming back to Staten Island. I don't know if someone drove me, or I drove myself, or if I walked.

I changed at some point into a soft dress. Dante's blood remains on my hands. Other than that, all I know is this view, my heartbeat in my ears, and the uncertain sense that everything has changed.

Dante is in a hospital somewhere. *I think.* Or he's dead in the back of an ambulance or the doctor's car. That knowledge washes over me numbly. An hour ago—a day ago, it would have rocked me to my core. *Torn me apart.* There's a real chance I'll never look into Dante's dark eyes and see love looking back at me again. I am alone in America. But in the wake of what he said, I can't shake the feeling I was alone in America already.

Christos is dead. That does ache. As much as I thought Luca killed him, part of me still hoped he was just hidden away in some basement, toiling until he got the chance to return to us. I didn't even get the chance to ask where Dante abandoned his body before the doctor rushed him away. Without conscious thought, I turn and leave the room, walk down the hallway until I reach Dante's door. It's closed. Dimly, I remember the threats not to enter without him, the intensity in his eyes. Was he hiding the manacles on his bed? The pictures? Or something worse?

I open the door and drift over to the wall of pictures. He didn't move the one of him and Christos. Did he trust me? Or was he just laughing at me behind my back? I pluck the picture off the wall and stare at it. How could I not have known Christos had fallen into this mafia mess? In the last year, after he dropped out of college, he was a little withdrawn, a little more snappish. Mama said that was because he was having a hard time figuring out what to do with his life. She said to give him space.

In the hollow of my chest, a small flame of frustration lights. That space may very well have been the thing that killed him. None of us knew. And I'd think getting involved with the mafia would be a diffi-cult, obvious process.

Unless the mafia smiled at you and asked your favorite memory of gyros.

I shake my head. That's…different. Right?

Somehow, I find myself wanting to know more about what happened between them. How they went from brothers in arms to enemies on opposite sides of a war. I leave Dante's room. My foot-steps echo on the wood floor, another reminder that I'm alone. I could call Mama, tell her it's safe to come home. But she'd ask, and I can't explain it all now. Not through the numbness blanketing my limbs, my tongue.

Do I owe Dante the same vengeance I meted out against Luca?

I open the door to Dante's office. If there are answers to be found in this house, they're in here. If they're not here, I'll bang on the doors to Piacere until they have to let me in and show me the basement I vaguely remember through a haze of alcohol. I'll shake them out of Seb, of Tony. They're somewhere. I just have to look.

Dante's desk beckons. I sit in his leather chair and inhale. His smell filters into my lungs, and something cracks within me. I clutch the picture of Christos so hard the paper crumples.

What am I doing? I'm a twenty-three-year-old waitress with two semesters of night school under my belt. I don't belong here. I only made sense in this world with Dante at my side, and now he's—

Tears sheet down my face. A whirlwind of emotions catches me in its hold, and I slump to the top of the desk, just shaking.

An engine roars up the drive outside, then a second one. Maybe I should just stay here, let whatever loose Lombardi or Coppola soldier find me to end the confusion.

No. Mama and Baba raised me better than that. Calimerises don't give up. I scrub the tears off my face and sit up just as the front door slams open.

"All right, let's whip this place into some kind of fucking shape," Uncle John says, his voice muted by the distance between Dante's office and the front foyer. "Where does Dino keep his papers?"

Someone replies. Maybe several someones. I can't make out the words.

"Because I'm *the fucking boss* now," Uncle John snaps.

"Dante and I have talked about this," Tony says so tightly I imagine him gritting his teeth. "If something happens to him—"

"Look, I love the kid, but you and I both know he's been off his game recently," Uncle John replies with vitriol. "Why don't we just—" He drops his voice lower, and I lose the ability to hear the conversation.

I strain to hear, but I can only make out the tone. Everybody sounds frustrated. Dante keeps a gun in his desk somewhere, I know. I open a drawer and rustle through. Nothing but stationery. The next drawer is all files. Footsteps approach me. This is taking too long. Dante would want his gun fast if he needed it. I run my hands along the underside of the desk and find a leather holster with a pistol.

The door bursts open. Uncle John stands there, with Tony and a few other men behind him.

"What the fuck are you doing behind Dino's desk?" he demands.

"I was—"

"Shut up." His face turns red as he whips around to Tony. "What the fuck is the Greek slut still doing in my nephew's chair? In his fucking house?"

The numbness creeps over me again. Dante's dead. He must be dead.

"Because she was captured earlier today," Tony replies. "And she's a Saint."

"*She's* a—" Uncle John's eyes bulge, and a vein leaps out on his neck. "No. No she's not. She's a fucking mistake you'd be dragging out by her hair if you had the sense God gave a brick." He advances toward me, wild with anger. "She ruined everything. She made Dino ruin everything. I told him, fucking warned him, that he was losing it. Shit, for all we know, she's a Lombardi plant. Wasn't her brother—"

His yelling turns to a roar in my ears that melds with my own heartbeat.

I don't think. I don't feel myself stand and raise the gun. I simply take aim, and fire.

Uncle John falls to the floor, blood splattering out of a hole in the center of his chest. Tony looks from the smoking gun to me, his eyes wide with mingled grief and shock.

I set the pistol down on the desk. The grip bears a bloody hand-print as I slowly sit down and clear my throat. "Is everyone ready to get to business now? Because we have a huge mess to clean up."

Find *Loved by the Mafia King: Mafia Kings Book 2 here.*

Desired by the Devil series

Whispers of the Devil

Banter of the Devil (coming soon)

The Mafia Kings series

Indebted to the Mafia King

Loved by the Mafia King (releases 9/15/2024)

Claimed by the Mafia King (releases 11/15/2024)

Sign up for Bella's newsletter here.

Follow Bella on Facebook here.

www.ingramcontent.com/pod-product-compliance
Lightning Source LLC
Chambersburg PA
CBHW070415310726
48977CB00003B/705